Fifties Chix: Third Time's a Charm

Angela Sage Larsen

HANDLEY REGIONAL LIBRARY
P.O. BOX 58
WINCHESTER, VA 22604

Published by Premiere

Published by Premiere
3131 Bascom Ave
Suite 150
Campbell CA 95008 USA
stwilson@fastpencil.com
408-540-7571
http://premiere.fastpencil.com

This is a work of fiction. The author makes many historical references, but encourages the reader to do her own research to learn about the twists and turns history has furnished to bring us to this: the future.

Printed in the United States of America.

First Edition

For Brooke

Acknowledgments

Like the Fifties Chix, I am just one of a team of multi-talented, fabulous individuals, including my brilliant and faithful editors Lori Van Houten and Liz Wallingford; my kind and wise agent, Bruce Butterfield; the incredibly capable and likable Fast-Pencil PREMIERE team; my advisor, helper and social media strategist genius, Marie Stroughter; my loyal and super-smart advisory board including René, Olivia, and Kaleigh; my Queen of Possibilities, Karen Hoffman; my Mastermind Group of accomplished women, especially Karen Conant. I have the best girlfriends in the world who continue to inspire me to create these characters. My gratitude for each of you knows no limit. I am also thankful for the Missouri Historical Society, a wonderful resource with knowledgeable and generous volunteers. You make me feel like a kid in a candy store when I visit!

Above all, I'm supremely blessed and grateful for a supportive family and my husband, Whit, who fathers these literary projects as much as I mother them.

Contents

Prologue ix

Chapter 1　Useless Generation 1

Chapter 2　Life is Like a Soap Opera 5

Chapter 3　Broken Family Trees 15

Chapter 4　Prodigal Sister 31

Chapter 5　Pilgrims and Strangers 43

Chapter 6　War and Peace 53

Chapter 7　Yours Truly, Anonymous 69

Chapter 8　Trading Off 81

Chapter 9　Down in Front 91

Chapter 10　Divided and Conquered 103

Chapter 11　"My Heart Shall not Fear . . . " 111

Chapter 12　That's How Rumors Get Started 119

Chapter 13　Make New Friends, Keep the Old 129

Chapter 14　Girl for Sale 141

Chapter 15　Friends and Faux 159

Chapter 16　If it's Broke, Fix it 171

Chapter 17　Run for Your Life 183

Chapter 18　Salvation of a Single Soul 193

Chapter 19　Willing Suspension of Disbelief 199

Chapter 20　Good as New 209

Epilogue 219

Glossary 221

Prologue

I am a success today because I had a friend
who believed in me and I didn't have the heart to let him down.
- Abraham Lincoln

1

Useless Generation

Useless Generation
By Miss Thurgood

"We will have to repent in this generation not merely for the vitriolic words and actions of the bad people, but for the appalling silence of the good people." - Martin Luther King, Jr.

When they look back on us in fifty-five years, what will they say about us? When the history books are written, what will they read about us? When they tell their grandchildren about us, what will they say? Will they say that ours was the generation who finally got it right?

Or will they say that in our generation, the division grew so great while no one watched that we broke in half?

Are we much better than our parents, or have we gone back in time?

I don't want to have my way if it means someone else suffers for it. I don't want to sleep undisturbed at night if there's a homeless person awake on the streets; a child going hungry; a man in jail for the color of his skin.

I do not want equality if it means the world has gone colorless. The blending of Black and White should not be a lifeless gray where there is no right or wrong; a fog of uncertainty that we are all in together, but where we can't see each other. Who is brave enough to reach out a trembling black or white hand to the black or white hand next to you? The colors in between are a full spectrum of hope, compassion, empathy, joy. When we clear the fog, a bow of hope lights our path to peace. If we stumble on the way to peace, we can still steady ourselves and find the way. But there is no stumbling where.

there are no steps forward, when we allow ourselves to be paralyzed by the haziness of the indifference, the intolerance, the ignorance, and worse of all, the complacency of this generation.

Until Whites stop living as if they set the standard for normal and everyone of color is abnormal, this generation and all the others following it will be useless. And until we all embrace the best of ourselves that our past has caused us to be, we can never have the humility to let go of our mistakes and accept our glorious future.

2

Life is Like a Soap Opera

May pulled the scratchy wool blanket closer. But she knew it wouldn't help; it wasn't the chilly November air that kept her shivering. It was knowing that when the clock struck midnight, she would risk everything for her friend. While she lay in bed in a well-appointed mansion, not daring to think of missing the Thanksgiving feast back home with her family, her friend was preparing an escape from the hands of a cruel slave master.

Normally, Marion "May" Boggs would not have been so brave; but tonight she would do anything for Emily. It had been her own fault, of that May was certain. The fact that Row hadn't tried to talk her out of it had only confirmed that May was indeed to blame. She didn't know if her actions tonight might rewrite history—might even rewrite Emily right out of her life; she did know that Crawford Dunkelman had a gun—and knew how to shoot it.

And she didn't know how three girls, three slaves, and a slave master's grand-baby were going to cross the Mississippi River in the middle of the night . . . she just knew they had to try.

With that, she swung her feet out of bed and folded the blanket. She was already dressed, even with her button-up shoes on. As the dark leather on the top of one of them caught a ray of moonlight, she thought with dread of her friend being beaten for wearing squeaky shoes and Marion's courage screwed up. She tore the sleeping cap from her hair, shoving it under her pillow, and marched with silent resolve to retrieve Rowena. But Row was waiting outside of Marion's door. Silently, she embraced Row. The thought of trying to do this without her was more than Marion could bear.

Perhaps Row felt the same because she hugged her friend back with the same strength.

For once, May Boggs was grateful that her wool overcoat was nearly threadbare. It was an unseasonably warm midwest day in November. She felt petty and even selfish for thinking it, but she hoped that the war being over might mean fewer sacrifices and maybe even a new coat. Once winter came hard in January, she'd be desperate for a new peacoat that didn't ride up her wrists or have patched-up seams. She nearly broke out into a sweat with the sun pulsing down on her through the naked tree branches and her quick pace to get home. She didn't want to miss a minute of "Pepper Young's Family," one of her favorite radio programs that started at 3:00 on the dot.

Whenever May dashed into the parlor of her family's brick bungalow and turned on the wooden tabletop radio with built-in speakers that looked like church windows, her mother would "tsk" and say radio stories weren't appropriate and demand May to turn it off at once. May would say, "I'm just checking the batteries" (which of course was somewhat nonsensical, because May presented it as some kind of a service instead of what it really was: running down the batteries), and her mother would consent with an impatient huff, as if the point was not worth arguing. And then May would curl up on the red velvet settee with the dark wood trim or help her mother prepare supper in the adjoining kitchen. Either way, they both listened together every day; but when asked, Mrs. Justine Boggs was happy to tell anyone how sinful soap operas were because they just promoted gossip, even if they were accounts of and by made-up characters.

May knew how important it was to her mother to appear a certain way and promote a virtuous image of herself and her family. Still, she wondered why it mattered . . . no one else seemed to mind soap operas, and the members in her mother's Lutheran Ladies church circle often compared notes about the radio stories. Usually Mrs. Boggs sat tight-lipped and solemn, even though May had a feeling her mother longed to jump into the conversation and hoot and coo and lament with the rest of them over Dwight and Carolyn Kramer on "The Right to Happiness" and how the Kramers could never find it. Her mother's dour temperament was one more thing that May didn't question. With America fighting the Second World War, everyone had made sacrifices and May just assumed that renouncing lightheartedness and simple pleasures was part of her family's contribution to the war effort.

Because of one of her best friends, Rowena Nolan, May well knew —at least from observation—what the war cost. So seeing her own mother, who had actually suffered so little in comparison to the Nolan family, walk the earth as if she carried a formidable burden, secretly irritated May and often caused tension in her own home. So that overly warm day in November, as May rushed home to hear her radio shows, her thoughts full of the recent past, she almost didn't notice on her way to the cabinet that the radio was already on.

"Now, hush, Marion, I knew you wouldn't want to miss anything." Mrs. Boggs smiled at her daughter, helping her off with her coat. Mrs. Boggs's stout, round features (that May's mirrored) for once seemed soft and warm and not at odds with her sharp demeanor.

May felt more reluctant to respond than if they were in a heated argument, so she didn't utter a peep, just walked to the adjoining kitchen to help peel potatoes. She realized that next to the sink full of potatoes was one of her mom's earthenware bowls filled with grated potato meat, which could only mean one thing: potato pancakes. A tear unexpectedly sprung to May's eye and she wiped quickly at her face. Her mother hadn't served Kartoffelpuffer, German potato pancakes, since America had joined the Allied forces against Germany and Japan. Mrs. Boggs avoided making the German dish as if by serving it to her family she was somehow in cahoots with the Germans. It was May's favorite food, if only because she was denied it, and it came to symbolize all the things sacrificed in the war. She couldn't help but glance at her shabby coat that her mom had just hung on a peg near the back door; maybe that new coat wasn't going to be just a mere fantasy after all.

❖   ❖   ❖

Dinner started out as a happy affair. Mr. Boggs, a history professor at a nearby college, always brought joy to the table with his *silly jokes and puns, interesting stories, and effusive affection for his family; but Mrs. Boggs in her infinite practicality always made sure to keep everyone firmly planted on Earth. That night, however, she seemed cheerful, almost frivolous. It was sinking in that the war was over, and May went along with her mother's good mood.*

"What did you learn in school, today Miss Marionberry?" May's dad asked, helping himself to more potato pancakes and heaping chunky homemade applesauce on top.

"We're starting our Thanksgiving and pilgrim theme," May said, smiling at the nickname her dad liked to use for her. "We're each supposed to do a family tree to see if anyone's relatives go back to the pilgrims and the Mayflower and all that." She scooped up the perfect bite with just the right amount of sour cream, apple, and pancake, but nearly choked at her mom's immediate and harsh response.

"That's a terrible idea! How does that help you learn anything? I don't want you doing that kind of nonsense; and certainly not at school for your teacher or other pupils to see!" Mrs. Bogg's fork clattered to her plate, making May jump and forget to enjoy her perfect bite.

In the kitchen, when the windows around them were squares of inky blackness at this winter hour, May worried that they were the only people in the world, a lonely feeling May got when her mother was irrationally upset like this. She wanted to escape, explore some happy, colorful, and exotic place, exist for no reason at all other than to just exist. Sometimes she even thought how nice it would be to be someone else for a day.

"Daddy?" May hoped her father could be a voice of reason.

Mr. Boggs didn't look at May, but kept his eyes on his wife. He gazed at her so tenderly, May was stunned. How did he continue to have such affection for such a sharp-edged woman? May of course loved her mother, but more often than not wished she could have a different kind of relationship with her. One like . . . well, one like Row had had with her mom before she took to bed and died of a broken heart. May felt inevitably guilty for wanting anything she didn't have, no matter what it was, and blushed as if her thoughts were obvious to everyone in the room.

"Justine," Mr. Boggs said gently to his wife.

"Now, Harold. I just don't like the idea is all. I don't know what is happening to our education system when we're forcing children to make silly charts instead of learning something useful. And she's in high school. That's a second grader's project." Mrs. Boggs got up from the table, tossing her embroidered napkin onto her empty chair. She grabbed the platter of remaining pancakes and took the plate from under her husband's nose. May could have had two more helpings, but her mother was declaring dinner officially over. In hopes of picking over the food, May got up to help with the dishes.

But her mother stopped her. "Marion, why don't you go see what Rowena is up to this evening? Lord knows she could use a friend right now."

"Right now" for the last two years, May thought.

May pushed her chair under the table, leaving her plate and napkin. As her mother turned to the sink, her dad gave May a reassuring wink.

"You need a nickel for a soda, kid?" he asked.

May's mother shook her head. She didn't say it out loud, but her thoughts could be inferred: We just had dinner, what does she need with a soda? May accepted her dad's offer and thanked him with a peck on the cheek on her way to retrieve her coat. It would be nice to buy her own soda for once; it was usually Rowena who had all the dough. For a long time, May had tried to keep track of her tab, but after it reached five dollars, she had given up. Row had said, "Don't worry, you can pay me back when you marry your prince and he abdicates his thrown for you," knowing how much May loved the romantic story of Wallis Simpson and the former King Edward.

"Thanks for dinner, Mom," May said.

"Don't stay out late," was Mrs. Boggs's reply.

May was relieved to be out of the house, not having noticed the stifling smell of heavy foods and the thin atmosphere of tension until she breathed in fresh air outdoors. Her huge orange cat Theo strutted over from his place on the porch for a quick pat before she left. Mrs. Boggs despised the cat and Theo preferred the outdoors anyway, but soon it would be too cold for Theo to be outside all night. May scratched his chin and felt his purring turn over like an old rusty motor. "You and I are going to stick together, aren't we, mister?" May said. She gave him one final pat and he sauntered back up the stairs to survey the neighborhood from his perch on the wide cement porch railing.

It had cooled considerably but was still a lovely evening for November. *Maybe we could just sit on the porch*, May mused on her way to Row's, brushing the cat hair off her coat.

Partway to her friend's house, under a flickering streetlight, she spotted Row coming her direction.

They barely said hi, just picked up where they left off at school.

"Did you listen?" May asked.

"Sure. They're never going to find happiness," Row said. It was customary for Row to say this line every time they compared notes on their radio shows and whenever they talked about "The Right to Happiness." Row asked, "Wanna grab a soda?"

"Let's get Em first."

"Of course; I'm not a chump!" Row snorted softly, looping her arm around May's.

May wanted to tell her about how strange her mother was acting, but it was hard to talk about her mom in front of Row, especially if it even hinted of complaint. May felt that having Emily there would soften the blow so she stayed quiet about it for the moment. It had been barely a year since Row's mother had died, and definitely not long enough to have adjusted to the new stepmother and stepsister who monopolized Row's father's attention.

The girls walked arm in arm the rest of the short distance to Em's, listening to the sounds of cars rushing by just a few blocks over. It seemed that since had Japan surrendered on V-J Day in August, more folks were out and about, feeling freer in their own skin. There was a long way to go to recovering, but the initial celebratory feeling hadn't worn off.

The dead leaves on the trees lining the streets rustled in a light breeze and they heard the yelling before they'd crossed the street to reach Em's block. They weren't surprised to find Emily sitting on the front step.

"I just knew you'd come," she said cheerily, bounding toward them in a graceful leap that only a ballerina could manage. She seemed so chipper, you would have thought her grandparents weren't screaming at each other in the brick house behind her.

"Sounds rough tonight," Row said. May wondered how she could say something so blunt but sound so soothing. If May had said that, she was certain it would have sounded like a criticism.

"Same old, same old," Em shrugged, tossing her dark hair carelessly. She stepped between the other two girls and linked arms with them.

"Are you alright?" May couldn't help but ask with concern in her voice.

"You worry too much," said Em in a laughing tone; but even in the evening darkness, May could tell that Em's eyes didn't reflect the mirth in her voice.

Row decided to change the subject. "Anyway, we're getting a soda and we can talk about this school project."

May's heart broke for her friends, she loved them so. She would trade places with them in an instant if she thought it would help. She never wanted to be without them.

3

Broken Family Trees

After Em and May teased Row about Tommy Twigler, the charming high school quarterback who was smitten with Row, Row changed the subject to their genealogy project for school. She didn't care much about old Twig anyway; he was too high on his horse for her taste. If he'd had such a rough upbringing, she wondered why he had to act so arrogant. She didn't have the patience for him.

"That assignment will be a breeze," Row said, slurping up the rest of her soda. "Mom kept trunkloads of family trees and genealogy stuff." They sat at their regular table at the diner and the owner, Bert, was waiting on them to leave so he could close up shop. He never kept regular hours; when it was slow, he closed and when it was busy, he stayed open till everyone left. The old man could be crotchety to May, Row, and Em, but they knew he liked them in his own way and they liked him back. They'd only been going there since the war; before that, one of Row's brothers would drive them to Ted Drewes for a frozen custard concrete.

"*Mother got bent out of shape when I brought it up,*" said May, introducing the subject of her mom for conversation. "*Why does she get like that?*"

Row said absently, "*Probably because your grandparents are German and she doesn't want everyone to know and think you are all secretly Nazis.*"

May laughed. "*How do you do that? Why, I'm sure you're right. I wonder why didn't I think of it myself.*"

"*Then why are my parents upset about it, Miss Know-it-all?*" Em turned to Row. She always referenced her maternal grandparents as her parents. Since her mother and father had been killed in an automobile accident when Emily was just a baby, Grandma and Grandpa Parks had raised her. Em blamed the frequent bickering at home on herself. Certainly her grandparents had felt imposed upon to have to care for an infant just when they thought they were finished with child-rearing and had already been struggling to make ends meet.

"*I know this one,*" May volunteered, pushing her empty soda glass toward the center of the table. "*They don't want to think about the past. Because it makes them sad.*"

In a rare moment of introspection, Em sighed, "*I'd like to know about the past, whether they want to talk about it or not. I'm glad we got this assignment.*"

"*Emily Jackson, am I to understand that you are happy to do schoolwork?*" Row teased, keeping the conversation from getting too heavy too fast.

"*Oh, hush!*" Em ran her finger along the rim of her glass to scoop up a trail of foam and dab on Row's nose. Row squealed and old Bert gave them The Look.

"Closing time," May agreed, nodding at Bert. They'd never been kicked out of Bert's and she didn't want to start a new trend.

The three girls walked back as slowly as they could without coming to a complete stop. Before they parted, Row invited them to a sleepover on Friday night, as usual.

Wednesday, November 14, 1945
Dear Diary,
I never knew a simple class project could cause so much controversy! Not knowing my true family history and Mother keeping it willfully from me is a travesty! Despite her unreasonable objections, I am having

Daddy sneak me family information right under Mother's nose. I wish she didn't have to make everything difficult, but the deceitful means I've resorted to are her own doing! I love her, as a daughter rightfully should love her mother. Certainly, I can't imagine life without my mother and don't wish to. I've seen with my own eyes, through the tragic experiences of my dear friends, Rowena and Emily, the effects of living motherlessly. Wouldn't it be wonderful if we could all just be happy? "The Right to Happiness," indeed, Diary! The funny thing is, Row and Em are always happy. I've never seen them so much as tear up. It's as if I've chosen to be sad on their behalf. This is why I proclaim here and now that what we all need is an escape...a grand adventure!

Daddy showed me an old mysterious letter box Mother keeps under the bed. There are some letters and even an old diary in German, but of course I don't understand those. Left to my imagination, I can only presume the letters have to do with romance, unrequited love, spies and intrigue! Also in the box are Mom's, Dad's and my birth certificates, my little baby brother's death certificate (rest his precious soul), a lovely pearl-encrusted pin and a gorgeous gold watch. It is a travesty of justice that Mother doesn't wear those jewels, that they are too fancy for her taste. OR...perhaps they are painful reminders of her romantic past. The watch must be German or something because it doesn't have a normal clock face (they tell time the same way in Germany, don't they?? A mystery that I am all too delighted to unravel!). All of these items I must view in secret and in haste, replacing them before Mother knows I've found them. Heck, I don't know why it matters, but I don't want to get Dad in trouble. I might just have to sneak the watch out overnight for the sleepover at Row's, though. The girls would really get a kick out of it. We promised Em we'd help with her family tree project. Her folks are being less helpful than Mother. Is it possible her parents are more difficult than mine? I sure have a long way to go before I find out if I'm related to any pilgrims! (Which of course, I'm not. Even though that would be so romantic and be such a great story! And frankly, if my assignment calls for being related to pilgrims, I'll find a way. Only you know, Diary, that it is probable that I am not. In the traditional sense, that is. And what a travesty, because it would be a wonderful story!)

Signed, Royally yours,

Lady Marion G. Boggs, the First

TWIG CAME BY TONIGHT. SAT ON THE PORCH FOR A WHILE, BUT I FIND HIM DULL. THEN PETEY DROPPED IN, MADE ME LAUGH AS USUAL AND TWIG GOT MAD AND LEFT. I'LL NEVER TELL MAY ABOUT TWIG...THINK SHE LIKES HIM. SHE SHOULD KNOW SHE'S NOT MISSING ANYTHING. HE JUST LIKES TO TALK ABOUT HIMSELF.

SCHOOL PROJECT. ALREADY DONE, THANKS TO MOM'S METICULOUS RECORD KEEPING. "METICULOUS" - THERE'S A WORD. YOU CAN TELL MAY IS STARTING TO RUB OFF ON ME!

WICKED STEPMOTHER GLADYS AND GRACE GOING TO THEIR FAMILY'S THIS WEEKEND, SO SLEEPOVER HERE WITH MY GIRLS JUST LIKE OLD TIMES. ALMOST JUST LIKE OLD TIMES. MISSED KELL TODAY. MISS HIM EVERYDAY. ORVAN AND WALLY, TOO. ALWAYS MISS MOM. AND EVEN THOUGH DAD'S STILL HERE, RIGHT UNDER MY NOSE, I MISS HIM MAYBE MOST OF ALL. WHERE WOULD I BE WITHOUT MY OLD MUTT FINIGAN AND MY BEST FRIENDS?

-ROWENA

WEDS. 11-14-45

Dear Diary,   Weds. Nov. 14, 1945

I can't wait to finish high school and get my own apartment. I'd like to work at a newspaper or as a telephone operator during the day and dance at night. I'll have to move far away because Mama and Papa would never let that happen. The first thing I'll do is research my real parents. Mama and Papa are doing the best they can, but they can't (no, won't) tell me anything about Mother and Father and the less they say the more I want to know. This is nothing new, it's just all coming up again with this family tree school theme. I've always wished I knew more about my parents, but now I realize how little I know about my father's family especially. The only thing I have is his last name. Do I have his eyes? His sense of humor? I haven't the foggiest idea.

Today at school Petey tripped and fell on his way to sharpening his pencil in composition class. He jumped right up and did a fancy little jetté with his legs and fluttered his arms like a ballerina. The whole class was laughing and he looked at me and said, "Did I do that right?" He is such a goof. It was the best laugh of the day!

~Emily

May couldn't breathe. She was holding her stomach and tears streamed down her face.

No one could get her laughing this hard except Em and Row. The two of them egged each other on until they got this response from her; and they were laughing pretty hard, too. Once Em had even wet her underwear, she was so hysterical. The girls gladly reminded her of this on just such an occasion, making them that much more frenzied.

May didn't even remember exactly what it was that had struck her funny bone, but she knew it felt good to laugh. What made it even better was how they all knew each other; they knew their quirks, their weaknesses, and even the tragedies of their respective pasts. But still they could find endless reasons to laugh.

May loved seeing them in the warm light of Row's room, like old times. Row's blonde hair fell in waves around her shoulders; May thought she looked like that old movie star, Veronica Lake. Row's natural beauty was never fussy; it was as effortless as . . . well, as Emily's. But Em's olive skin, dark eyes, and black hair were a contrast to Row's. Row was even taller and lankier than Em and May. May noticed that the girls at school that clustered together often looked alike, but not May and her friends. They were a motley trio.

As they tried to catch their breath, happily exhausted, May let herself flop onto her back, wiping tears from her face. She was brimming with affection for her friends. No matter what life or family threw at them, they'd always have each other. She'd grown up feeling lonely, envious of classmates with multiple siblings and aunts, uncles, and grandparents all living under one roof mostly because of the Depression. Her home wasn't unhappy, per se, just . . . well, lifeless. Even her cat wasn't interested in snuggling up or being part of her life like Finigan was with Row. She craved romance and adventure, but had never had a boyfriend or been out of Missouri. Her diary was riddled with novels that she started to write, but couldn't finish. If she couldn't even finish an imaginary scenario, how could she live out a real one? She read every book she could get her hands on, from A Tree Grows in Brooklyn to Wuthering Heights to serials in the magazines. She even read history, trying to envision herself in another place and time. But these moments, with her friends at her side, she never longed to be anywhere else.

"Let's be friends forever," May said, in a more serious tone than fit the mood, but in her typical dramatic fashion.

"Done," Row agreed easily.

"Where do you think we'll be in fifty years?" mused Em after she too agreed to a lifelong friendship.

"Mrs. Rowena Twigler will have a household of kids is my guess," giggled May.

Row tossed a pillow at May. "No, thank you! Besides, I thought you liked Twig, May."

May did secretly fancy Tommy, but not for his good looks, athletic talent, and extraordinary popularity. May saw his intelligence, which no one else seemed to appreciate. He was creative and smart, but hid behind all the other stuff. In a way, May was almost envious of him. She didn't have anything to hide behind. What you saw is what you got with Marion Boggs.

"She's got bigger fish to fry, like Wallis Simpson did," Em said, referencing May's dream of marrying into royalty.

Row glanced around the room then, wondering about her home in fifty years and who would be living here. For the moment, everything looked to be in its right place: her room was "hospital" clean, as her stepmother Gladys called it, thanks to the housekeeper she brought in; Row's—or rather, her brothers'—big German shepherd, Finigan, snoozed in the corner at the foot of Row's bed. Row's mother had allowed the Rin Tin Tin twin to sleep in Row's room, but often, Row's father had kicked the dog out, insisting that animals should live outside. Since her mother had died, however, Row noticed that Finigan was always inside without any objection from Dad. Gladys had complained about it once, but a private conversation must have been had between Row's father and Gladys because it was never mentioned again. Row didn't remember a time when Finigan wasn't around; Fin and this big old house were the only constants in Row's life, the only charms remaining from her once charmed life.

And recently, Row had found out more about the history of this home, which had been in her family for nearly one hundred years. Her parents had frequently spoken of the house with such reverent and affectionate tones, the house seemed like a large, silent, everpresent member of the family. But they had neglected to fill in some of the darker features of the house's history; like how after Ronan

O'Rourke had migrated to New York from Ireland, married his bride, Bryna, and moved to Missouri in 1850, building her a lovely farmstead where their baby daughter Fiona would be born a year later (facts Row knew by heart), Ronan and Bryna were tragically killed by disease, orphaning their infant daughter. Yes, her parents had skipped the sad part of the story and now that Row had discovered the truth, she had a nagging feeling that the house might not be as charmed as she once thought. In fact, thinking of her mother's passing in the room down the hall, Row wondered if the house was partly to blame, carrying a curse all these years later. And perhaps Bryna or Ronan or both had died in the exact same room as her mother. But these were exactly the kinds of things she didn't speak about. They might be May's style of story-telling, and maybe even Em's, but it wasn't like Row to dwell on these kinds of things or extrapolate facts into wild fantasies. Besides all that, Row didn't like to burden people with her fears or foibles, she preferred to keep it light. So she kept her mouth shut.

May rolled onto her side and looked dreamily at Em, who was propped up against the double bed in Row's bedroom. "Where will you be in fifty years, Em? Dancing in New York?"

"Not when I'm sixty-five, silly! Besides, right now I'm more interested in where I came from than where I'm going." She let out a long dramatic sigh. "Want to hear what I found out at the library after school today?"

The other two girls sat up in eager anticipation. "Of course!" May said.

Row was relieved to have her mind occupied with someone else's news. "Are you related to a pilgrim?" she joked.

"I didn't quite get that far back," Em said. "But I found an old newspaper referencing my parents' car accident."

Row and May gasped simultaneously.

"They listed my dad's grandfather as a survivor; the article said his name was Noah Jackson. Why wouldn't my mother's parents tell me that and why haven't I seen anyone from that side of the family?"

"What else did it say? Is Noah still alive? Did it mention your dad's parents?" Row asked.

"My dad's parents were Roberta and Judah. Other than that, I couldn't find any information about Noah—my great-grandfather —at all. The article didn't even mention me as a survivor." A cloud of sadness that was heartbreaking to behold passed over Emily's brown eyes. May worried she might see Em cry for the first time and felt awful that this had come so quickly after such merriment just moments before. "I'm not going to find out if I'm related to a pilgrim. I don't have any family who cares. My grandparents were stuck with me; no one else wanted me or came forward to see me or be part of my life!" Em spoke as if realizing the impact of the words as they came out and her eyes glistened.

"Em, shhh . . . ." Row leaned over and hugged her friend.

"Forget the assignment, Em. I'll make up your family tree if I have to. I'll make sure you're related to twelve pilgrims if you want," May said passionately.

Em and Row looked at May and a smirk appeared on Row's lips. "What?" May demanded. And then Em smirked, too. A moment later they were giggling.

"What?" May asked again.

"Just . . . you. Thank you. Thanks for being willing to create a family tree for me," Em said. She wanted to add, *Thanks for being naïve enough to think that would help*, but she didn't want to be insulting. What May said was sweet.

May couldn't help but think of her own family tree. She might be having to conjure up a family history herself if she couldn't get more information from her dad.

"Oh!" May exclaimed, remembering what she had brought to show the girls. It would be the perfect distraction. May scrambled to her feet, while Finigan thumped his tail, pleased with any activity in his vicinity. May gave the dog a quick pat and went to her overnight bag next to the warm radiator to retrieve the watch. With a reverent tenderness, May placed the gold watch on her wrist and turned to present it to them, her face glowing.

The watch had the desired effect; Em and Row scooted closer to her and reached out to touch the shining gold-embellished clock face. Their eyes were wide with surprise. Row's right hand went instinctively to the tiny white gold heart that hung on a fine chain around her neck. She was not the kind of girl to be impressed by jewelry, but the watch May presented felt special, like the pendant that rested against her throat.

"What's the story behind this watch?" Em breathed in hushed tones, as if a louder voice would leave a mark on the delicate design. "The fact that your parents never sold it for money must mean it's pretty special."

"I thought the same thing," May agreed. "They don't know I took it . . . I'm just borrowing it and I'll put it back tomorrow. But I'll have to ask Daddy what he knows about it."

"Where do you wind it?" Em asked and May shrugged, having wondered the same thing.

"Is it engraved?" Row wondered, looking at it closely.

May removed the watch and turned it over. Sure enough, in subtle script etched on the back, were the words, Liebe kann nicht nach der Zeit enthalten sein. Die Liebe ist ewig.

Em inhaled softly. "It looks like gibberish."

"It's not gibberish—" Row started.

"—it's German," finished May. "Anyone speak German?"

"Your mother," offered Row. The girls giggled. A lot of good it would do to ask Mrs. Boggs, from whom May had stolen—er, borrowed—the watch.

After fawning over the wristwatch, searching for a way to wind it or set the hands to the right time, and fantasizing about its backstory for forty-five minutes, the girls were ready to hit the hay. Instead of placing it back safe in her overnight case, May kept the watch on and wrapped her other hand around it. She didn't want to give it back, but tonight she didn't have to. She thought of the heart that Row wore. Row had refused to talk about it even when May asked if it was a locket and what was inside. Maybe Row needed a secret; the whole town knew she had lost three brothers in the war and a mother as a result. There had been weeks and weeks' worth of newspaper articles and stories about Row and her father, and Row was something of a "celebrity" around town. She couldn't go to the grocery or the diner without someone recognizing her, whispering softly and "tsk"ing sadly. If that pendant was something Row had control over and didn't have to talk about if she didn't want to, May could respect that. Or she could try to.

As the radiator rattled to a stop and the house became quiet with the night, May realized she could hear the ticking of the watch. It was curious, though, it didn't sound like it kept proper time. It seemed to beat in time with her heart, a tick-tick instead of a steady tick per second. She shouldn't be surprised that it wouldn't function properly; it was obviously quite old. And without a way to wind it, it was sure to conk out soon.

As she let herself be soothed by the heartbeat of the watch, her thoughts drifted to Emily and their earlier conversation. Soon May's thoughts distilled down to a single refrain: *We've got to help her find Noah Jackson. Not just for the school assignment, but maybe it would help Em find some peace about her family background.*

May was carried away by the mantra to a deep sleep, a dark and comfortable place so restful that she didn't even budge until the crow of a rooster roused her to a sitting position in the morning.

In 1864.

4

Prodigal Sister

Maxine Marshall waved goodbye to her friends all spilling out of the open windows of James O'Grady's car as it pulled away from the front of her house. She felt elated, free, giddy. She didn't know the last time she'd felt that way, if ever. There was no particular reason for it, really. Their circumstances hadn't changed. But for the first time, she felt like the five of them—Ann, Judy, Bev, Mary, and herself—and even James were really friends now. They had just spent the evening at a fifties-themed diner that Mary had discovered and Maxine had allowed herself the fantasy that they were back in 1955 with a few significant differences: they were all friends (instead of being forced together by circumstances out of their control) and . . . they weren't facing a circumstance that was out of their control.

She was still laughing to herself as she swung the front door open, vowing to stay this lighthearted over the next several days. Certainly there was a solution coming and even if it took longer than she thought it would, she could at least enjoy the ride—

"Max!"

"Mel??" The unexpected sight of Maxine's college-age sister, Melba, standing in the living room brought a new wave of joy that nearly knocked Maxine over.

They rushed to each other and embraced while their parents, to whom Melba had just been speaking, looked on happily.

When Melba pulled back, Maxine clung on. The last time she'd seen Melba had been during Christmas break in 1954. In the meantime, Maxine had time-traveled to this strange dimension. Whether it felt like sixty years ago or six months ago, Maxine wasn't sure. A sob bubbled in her, but Maxine wasn't a crier in public—even if the public was her family—so the cry came out as a laugh instead.

"Hey," Melba said, half-smiling, half-concerned.

"It was a lot harder having you away at college than I thought," Maxine said, finally finding the will to let go of her sister. Melba looked as beautiful and assured as ever, but her hair was different. Instead of the big smooth curls both girls worked so hard to get with stinging chemicals and burning heat and pinching rollers in the 1950s, Melba now wore her hair in a natural afro and the tiny ringlets radiated out from her head like a magnificent crown of energy. It fit Maxine's daring, beautiful sister to a T. Every Friday night Maxine had gone with her mama—and Melba before she went off to college—to her church friend Nan's grandma's house, where they'd meet up with all the church ladies and do their hair for the week. Now here in the future, Friday nights were unscheduled. Gloria Marshall had her hair done in a salon during the day. And Maxine was left to her own devices with her 1950s cut. She wished she could just wear braids and a kerchief, like her mama had done toward the end of the week before beauty parlor night.

Growing up, it had been Melba who was outspoken and brazen. In Maxine's eyes, Mel could do no wrong. At a young age, Mel had vowed to go to college and "get out of this Godforsaken place." She didn't intend to live a tentative life as a colored woman in a volatile town. Maxine had thought Melba was a hero for having such a lofty goal; but their parents had tempered Mel's enthusiasm, assuring her that she would have to deal with prejudice wherever she ended up and that her being educated wouldn't make everyone else less ignorant—or make the world a safer place for a colored woman.

When Maxine was much younger, she had thought their mama looked gorgeous in her crisp maid's uniform—the stark and stiff pale blue and bright white cotton contrasting appealingly against Mama's flawless deep-toned skin—until Mel had accused Mama of being a willing slave in uniform to the Johnsons. Mel and Mama had been having a fight like only Mel and Mama could, but Mel's disrespectful irreverence and thoughtlessness had gone too far. Mel had sobbed an apology soon after, but her awful comment had made Maxine question things about her mother and her mother's job she hadn't noticed before. And she started to wonder what her mother would have done with her life if she'd had more choices.

Maxine was getting a peek now in this sudden shift to the future. Both of her parents had different jobs, better jobs, but Maxine worried it still wasn't good enough. Her mama was bigger than life.

Those years before Melba left for college had been filled with painful bouts that were enough to tear the family right apart, yet

Maxine was secretly jealous of the rows. There was no fire or spark between her and her parents. She never did anything bold or rebellious enough to get them fired up like Mel did. Partly because she respected her parents and she understood it wasn't her place to question how they cared for her and she didn't want them to worry about her and her safety. But partly because she didn't have the courage. That's why Maxine loved writing so much. She could write all her questions, fears, doubts—even her good ideas—without offending anyone or causing waves or pulling her parents' attention away from bigger issues.

The quill on paper was a safe place.

Sometimes, Maxine thought, she was too safe, to the point of being invisible. Maxine's traveling to this new dimension had apparently entirely escaped her parents' notice. Did it escape their observation that she was from another era? Could they not see that she was an even bigger misfit than before?

Maybe now that Mel was back for the summer, things would be different . . . or rather, the same again. Maxine struggled to know if that was what she wanted.

As Maxine clung to her big sister in a welcome-home hug, Mama joined the circle, squeezing the girls together. "Go get settled, Mel, and we'll have a real family dinner."

"I already ate, Mom, and I'm meeting friends anyway," Melba said. She wore huge gold hoop earrings and Maxine couldn't look away from her. She seemed so self-assured, gorgeous, and . . . mature, even more than usual. So quickly after her vow moments before to remain happy, Maxine felt something tug at her. A familiar feeling: loneliness. Even right here, surrounded by her family. Future-Melba was different, just like everyone else.

"Come on, Max, let's check out the damage you did to our room." Melba smiled at Maxine with her lips, but her eyes told another story. There was a distance between the sisters that Maxine could feel.

Maxine lugged one of her sister's bags to their shared room and once in, Melba closed the door behind them and her disposition changed to match the coolness Maxine had felt.

"I'm glad to see you, really, but we need to talk. Did you write this?" Melba pulled *The Invisible Truth* out from a large purse that hung at her side.

Maxine felt blindsided by the sudden shift in Melba's mood and her mind whirled as she tried to figure out how Melba would have a copy of the underground school rag and know that Maxine had a hand in any part of it.

"It's—it's—an underground school paper—"

"I know what it *is*, Maxine. I went to that high school, too, remember?" She put her hand on her hip in that maternal way and with the other hand, like a magic trick, flipped the paper open to the essay Maxine had written, "Useless Generation."

"How—"

"Conrad, that's how." Melba outed the girls' cousin. "Besides that, it doesn't take a rocket scientist to figure out who 'Miss Thurgood' is." Melba referenced the pen name Maxine had used in attempt to remain anonymous. "Thurgood Marshall? You don't have to be a genius to crack that code."

Melba's eyes burned into Maxine and Maxine faltered. She was baffled. Why was Melba so bent out of shape? Maxine was sure that this was one thing that her big sister would have been proud of. Wasn't it just like Mel to have written an essay like Maxine had?

"What if I did write it?" Maxine demanded, feeling her defenses rise, along with a flash of frustration, disguised as anger.

"This is very inflammatory stuff, Max. You can't think people are going to read this and not get riled up. And you're putting yourself right in the middle of it."

Since when was it a priority of Mel's to not get folks riled up? Maxine wondered. She thought of the time Melba had announced her crush on Marcus Hansen, a handsome, wealthy, and popular football player. Who was white. So white, his hair and skin were the same pale peachy-yellow shade, barely even a color at all. Melba had kept their secret relationship under wraps and her parents made sure of that. It wasn't that it was distasteful or frowned upon; it was a matter of life and death. For two weeks, no matter how late it was when either of their parents got home, they had found the energy to battle with Melba. Of course, no one had asked Maxine what she thought, even though Mama said it was "family business." "Every decision you girls make affects this family and makes it our business. This can't end well, Melba! You're putting you, your family, and your little sister in jeopardy."

At least after the first night of arguing Mama hadn't repeated "Know your place." That had sent Melba into a tizzy like Maxine had never seen before. Maxine wasn't sure why. It seemed like "knowing your place" was a comforting thing. And besides, hadn't they revered her great-grandmother Gin's words, "When everyone know they place, they happy"?

One day the fighting had just stopped. Melba had brought home a new boyfriend. His name was Cooper Brown and even his last name was assuring to Mama and Daddy. Like Marcus, Cooper was handsome, popular and athletic. He wasn't as wealthy as Mark, but his daddy was a preacher at the Baptist church they attended. Cooper was colored and went to the colored school.

Mel had fallen for Cooper quickly. It was as if Marcus Hansen had never existed. Mark had telephoned the house once when Mel was out. Mel wasn't even with Cooper, but Maxine had heard her mom, who had pretended not to know who Marcus was, tell him pointedly, "Melba is out with her new colored boyfriend." It was the first and last time Marcus had called. Maxine had felt sorry for him, scared for her sister, and unsettled by the whole thing. But again . . . no one had asked her what she thought.

Now, in their shared-again bright yellow bedroom, Maxine's resolve to be happy dissolved along with her will to defend herself against Mel's accusatory tone. As usual, she couldn't match Mel's combative spirit. Besides, Maxine wasn't sure what she was defending. She took a few steps back and sat on her bed. "What's so bad about it?" she asked about her essay. "It's . . . the *future*. Now. I mean, it's not like it's . . . 1955." She nearly choked on the words. How many times had she wanted to talk to Melba over the past few weeks and tell her that Maxine and her friends had time-traveled and that she felt lost and alone? Too many to count.

"Just because we've come a long way, doesn't mean we don't still have a long way to go. If I learned one thing my first year in college, it's that."

Maxine hung her head. She was feeling a full range of emotion in a very short amount of time, and now she was feeling embarrassment. She never wanted her big sister, her heroic sister, to be disappointed in her. She knew though that it wasn't Mel's first year in college that had taught her that there was "still a long way to go." It was what had happened to Cooper Brown before Melba had even been accepted to college.

"Listen to this, Mel. You wrote: *The blending of Black and White should not be a lifeless gray where there is no right or wrong; a fog of uncertainty that we are all in together, but where we can't see each other.* Tell me something," Melba asked Maxine in a quieter tone, "Just who are you mad at? Whites or Blacks?"

Without thinking, Maxine answered, "I guess both a little."

"Well, if anything you're a good writer . . . because that definitely comes through."

Maxine wondered, and almost asked out loud, if Cooper was still in jail like he had been in 1955 for a crime he didn't commit. But she thought better of asking and went back to her customary silence.

❖　❖　❖

Ann lifted the delicate gold chain from its box on her dresser and as she raised it high enough, the charm swung free. Her tatty had given her a gold Star of David, and probably at great expense, for her Bat Mitzvah, but she had made it a policy to not wear it in public other than to temple. She wasn't sure what it was about the weekend and the night before—was it meeting with Mrs. Fairview, was it letting go of James O'Grady, was it allowing herself a fun evening with her best friends? Maybe . . . mostly, though, it was Maxine's courage to write what she had written for *The Invisible Truth*—but suddenly she felt impelled to wear the necklace. Maybe she was testing her friends. Maybe being bold about her beliefs instead of being quiet and retiring, as she often was about most things, would help her discover just how true these friends really were.

Or maybe she just needed a reminder of something sacred close to her heart in this brash, chaotic, often unholy new world. Last night she had discovered a stack of magazines in the living room; they were party planning magazines with headlines like, "Amaze your Guests!" "Add Thrills to Your Mitvah Event!" "What's Cool and What's Hot for Bar/Bat Mitzvah Now!" Ann's tummy had done an uncomfortable flip flop as she had thought of her little brother's Bar Mitzvah in another year or so in terms of a circus act of some kind. She'd been fingering through the magazine when her mom had walked in.

"Never too soon to start planning!" Kat had grinned at her daughter.

Ann had smiled uneasily at her mom and glanced back down at a picture of half a large sinking ship (could that be the *Titanic*?) as the background of a big spectacular Bar Mitzvah party. Among many of Ann's thoughts, one had been, *How can my parents afford something like this for Alex?*

As if reading her mind, her mom had said, "It only happens once. But don't worry, we're saving money by not hiring a party planner."

Ann came back to herself on Monday morning holding the beautiful pendant her father had given her, her mom's words still echoing in her ears. She wanted to look forward to this day, turning over a new leaf and seeing her favorite teacher, Mrs. Fairview, back in school again. She felt ashamed in God's eyes, embarrassed about her family's new ambivalence about religion, and so put the incident the night before out of her mind—

deciding to be content to wear what was in her heart around her neck.

❖   ❖   ❖

Judy glanced around her fifth period currents events class and sighed happily. There were her best friends, Bev, Mary, Maxine, and Ann, surrounding her, and at the head of the class—where she belonged—her favorite teacher Mrs. Fairview. Judy was starting to like the future; when she had woken up on May 5th fifty-five years after she'd fallen asleep one night, she had been rattled to say the least. But she was starting to adjust to the technology and new social customs, and she was growing closer to the friends who had this strange phenomena in common with her. And her teacher, who had gone missing last week, was back in their lives, giving Judy a sense of comfort that had been missing, like someone had hidden her security blanket but had given it back after a long absence.

And . . . there was Bob Jenkins.

Secretly—or not so secretly—it all came down to Bob Jenkins. He had been to her house, complimented a picture of her with her war hero father, messaged her on Facebook, and called to her when he'd been hurt in a baseball game over the weekend. And beyond that, he was just downright dreamy. She hadn't seen him yet today, but the day wasn't over. She was filled with anticipation.

As her gaze passed over her friends, she expected to see the same jubilation in their expressions, but was shocked to discover they were not on the same page. Ann, not surprisingly, was staring out the window in her typical daydream trance. Bev, in her letterman's sweater and sneakers, was gathering papers she'd scattered on her way into the classroom and repeatedly glancing toward the back of the class over her shoulder. Maxine kept her dark eyes down and chewed nervously on her pinky nail. Mary, in her usual clean and perky ponytail and cat-eye glasses, seemed almost sad. This astonished Judy most of all; Mary had just spent the previous evening with her dreamboat, James O'Grady. In fact, they had all been together. Mary should have been glowing.

Sure, Mary had returned the mechanical baby she'd toted around all last week for a school project, but she had been looking forward to getting rid of the thing, or so Judy thought. As Judy considered what could possibly be going on with her friends, the class bell rang and before Mrs. Fairview could even begin to address the class, one of the student's hands shot up.

Not waiting to be called on, the student, a know-it-all named Dan Henderson, demanded of Mrs. Fairview, "Can we talk about this racist article in *The Invisible Truth?*"

"Dan!" Some of the students protested his direct reference of the underground school newspaper to a teacher. Others, though, agreed with Dan and still others muttered, "It was racist?"

"I take it you've all read the article, then?" Mrs. Fairview asked, careful to keep her eyes averted from Maxine. No *Welcome backs* or *Where were you?*s today.

Answering her question indirectly, the classroom filled with a dull roar, everyone speaking at once. The title of the article in question, "Useless Generation," bopped about the room like a beach ball over a crowd of beach-goers.

The last thing Mary wanted to talk about was *The Invisible Truth*. She had found a poem in it just last night that she suspected was about her. Ann and Judy looked around the classroom, a bit confounded, as they had read the essay and found nothing wrong with it. Bev shook her head at all the fuss. *Why can't everyone just have a rational discussion?* Maxine's cousin Conrad, who sat in the back of the classroom, was wondering the same thing.

It was only Maxine who had no reaction at all and kept her focus on her desk.

"We should be allowed to know who wrote it!" someone called out.

Mrs. Fairview calmly explained, "These pieces are written anonymously for a reason . . . but that can't stop us from discussing—"

Before she'd finished speaking, another student accused loudly, "It was her. Maxine Marshall wrote it! Diane Dunkelman told me."

Maxine felt all the eyes in the classroom on her, but there were four pair of eyes she was particularly conscious of: Ann's, Mary's, Judy's, and Beverly's.

5

Pilgrims and Strangers

Mrs. Marion Fairview, the former Miss May Boggs, had been thinking incessantly about her old friend Emily and their— May's, Row's, and Em's—first time travel adventure together. May had known so little about the watch and how it worked. She hadn't known how to control where to go, whom to go with, and how to take what was needed. The knowledge she had now, improved though still imperfect, was cold comfort without her friend at her side. For years, she had tried to put Em out of her mind because missing her hurt too much. After many attempts at finding her, May and Row had finally given up. Or, as they told themselves, put the search on temporary hold. But the years had stretched out, life had moved on, and May experienced adventures she could not have imagined. The memory of Em nearly faded into the background. But now, with these five girls at the center of her life, and especially with what Maxine was enduring, Emily Jackson seemed to be related to almost every thought May had.

It was time to try to find Em again.

So May spent every free moment going back in her mind to that first escapade with the gold watch in 1945. When she, Em, and Row had woken up in Row's farmhouse in 1864, it had seemed that they had been thrust into a grand escapade. But things had ended uncertainly and Em would never be the same afterward. May was sure if she could comb over every detail she could remember, she might find the key to finding Emily and helping her come back to them all these years later.

❖   ❖   ❖

May rubbed her eyes and stretched. Hearing the rooster crow from Row's backyard, through a big yawn, May asked, "When did you get a rooster?" As she adjusted to the light of dawn, snippets of the enjoyable evening before with her friends coming to her in flashes, she caught a glimpse of Row, who seemed uncharacteristically discombobulated. May made out Emily behind Rowena; Em was a blur of activity, folding blankets, retrieving her overnight things as if there were a fire.

"Is that bacon I smell cooking? Is your dad—?"

Row whispered fiercely, "I don't know if it's my dad. He doesn't cook. And we don't have a rooster, Marion. Something strange is happening!"

"Why—" May noticed Row's room felt different. She suddenly became wide awake. "What's going on?"

"We don't know. But get up, find your clothes and get dressed. Now." It wasn't like Row to be so bossy. May didn't know if she liked it. But she had no time to decide.

"We're getting out of here. We're going to your house," Em told May, in the same kind of desperate whisper Row was using.

"*Why* my house?"

Row and Em stopped searching for their clothes for a long second to look at May. Row said, "Because nothing ever changes at your house."

The rooster crowed again, accompanied by an immense rumble and rattling sound.

"What in the world . . . ?" Row ran to the window and stared. Her normally creamy complexion went pasty. May and Em, still in their nightgowns, scrambled to see what she was looking at and May's mouth fell open.

"Is that a . . . wagon?" May asked stupidly. It was obviously a wagon. With two horses and a farmer. She found herself shaking her head, as if she could repair something that had come loose.

"I know what this is, I know what this is!" Row seemed suddenly delighted and relieved. "This is a dream. Of course. This is a dream. Alright, I'm just going to enjoy it. It's weird, but it's interesting."

"Whose dream?" Em asked.

"Mine," all three girls said simultaneously.

"Jinx!" May said automatically. She was always last to say it, but realized that now might not be the time to be triumphant at their jinx game. Figures, when she was the one to call it. Em and Row just as automatically linked fingers and each said a poet's name to remove the "jinx."

"Elizabeth Barrett Browing," mumbled Em.

"Emily Dickinson," declared Row, naming the poet May always used.

Suddenly, Row's bedroom door burst open.

"Well, good, at least you're up!" a tall sturdy woman with a thick Irish accent declared. She wore a long skirt and over it a large oversized white apron. The girls gaped at her in shock. The woman glanced over them and then pointed to Em. "I only needed two helpers; is one of you for the Jackson farm? I don't like the thought of it any more than you do—but I won't be gettin' in trouble for you —so you best head back over there to Shelby Jackson before he comes lookin' for you. Or worse . . . that Willimina comes." She shuddered to herself, almost comically. Then her attention came back to the girls in the room, "Get movin'!"

"Yes, ma'am." It was Row who spoke, and then followed with a nervous curtsy.

The woman laughed a hearty but pleasantly melodious roar at Row's formal gesture. She gathered a blanket sitting on a chair near the door and stepped back out.

Once she was down the hall bellowing at someone else, Row murmured, "I don't believe it. My dream is getting weirder. I think that was my great-grandmother. Who does she think we are?"

Still convinced it was her own dream and not Row's or Em's, May wondered why she would be dreaming about Row's grandma, while Em wondered how Row wouldn't know that her great-grandmother was visiting.

And also why her great-grandmother looked like she was in her twenties.

"I say we all pinch each other and whomever's dreaming will wake up," May suggested.

"I don't want to wake up yet . . . I'm curious about Shelby Jackson. He could be a member of my family!" Em gasped. The mischievous sparkle in her eye that had been missing last night was back, and it was hard to resist.

"Let's go find him," Row said.

"Yeah, nobody wake up till we find him," agreed May. Then she giggled. Now she knew it was all dream because only in a dream would she say something so absurd.

They crept downstairs, hoping to avoid Row's maybe-great-grandmother, but she rounded into the parlor from the kitchen.

"What do you have on? You're not going out half-clothed," the woman bellowed, looking them up and down. "I've taken in some sewing; you'll just have to wear some of those things for now."

The three girls stood frozen, Row taking in her surroundings. What used to be the parlor in her home smelled of new wood and fireplace smoke. There was an unrecognizable mauve wallpaper on the walls and the room was arranged oddly with unfamiliar furniture. Row wanted to point out a fireplace that was naked brick; in her house, the brick had been painted a dark ivory. As her mind raced to make sense of it all, the woman returned with piles of old-fashioned clothing.

"Now get dressed and stop frittering the whole day away. You." She pointed at Row purposefully. "You are going to help me take care of the baby."

Row's mouth popped open. She wasn't exactly the mothering type. That would be May. May was responsible and loved children —

"Go on," urged the strawberry blond force of nature, waving off May and Emily. "Give my regards to that sweet Mrs. Daisy if you see her," she said aloud and then muttered to herself, "She has her hands about as full as I do."

The girls quickly scrambled to put on the clothes they were given, heavy floor-length skirts and fussy cotton blouses. Row looked goofy because she was too tall and too skinny for her skirt.

"Someone trade with me," she whispered loudly, glancing at the other girls. Em and May couldn't help but giggle at Row. She always had looked put together. Until now. Her skirt sagged at the waist and the hem drooped just below her shins.

"There he is!" called out the lady from the next room as they heard a baby cry.

"That's your cue." Emily pushed Row playfully.

"I don't like this. Not just because of the baby," Row clarified. "I just think we should stay together."

"Missy, Jacob is crying for you," urged the woman. "Bring him to the kitchen for me."

"Jacob . . . is my grandfather," wheezed Row, barely loud enough for the girls to hear.

A trickle of fear slithered down May's spine. This was already longer and more detailed than any dream she'd ever had.

"Go take care of the baby—uh, your granddad—while we go try to find Shelby Jackson and see if he's related to Noah Jackson. And then we'll wake up, or get out of here," Emily directed. "We'll be right back." Her curiosity and sense of adventure had gotten the best of her.

As Em and May closed the front door behind them, May caught a last glimpse of Row. She seemed terrified. The trickle of fear May had felt suddenly seemed a flood.

Once outside, Em laughed out loud and linked her arm to May's as she so often did. "Look at this, Marion! Look where we are!"

May looked. What had once been a neighborhood of bungalows from the 1920s was now a cow pasture and fields of dormant, gray-colored stalks. May wanted to find her neighborhood now, see if her house even existed. Her throat felt sore from sudden anxiety. But the more full of dread May felt, the more pleased as punch Em seemed.

"I have to tell you something," May said, tightening Em's arm to her side. "I think this is my fault." She felt the watch under the long sleeve of her "new" blouse. The watch felt warm, heavy, out of place. "I think the watch did this."

Em stopped in her tracks, her eyes still sparkling. "Oh, May, don't tell me you believe this is all real?"

The sun rose higher in the sky, but a bitter wind kicked up, carrying away any warmth the sun may have offered. The tobacco field, long since harvested and cut down, rattled in the wind as if it was chattering with the cold. The air smelled of slightly damp earth, wood and manure. It also carried the timeless scent of approaching winter.

"I kept thinking of Noah Jackson and how I wished we could find him . . . and we woke up here. Now. Or—then," May corrected. It sounded crazy. But it was happening, wasn't it? Even though the words came out tentatively, she knew she was right.

"Well, we'll just have to enjoy it. It's the adventure we've always been looking for!" Em resolved to enjoy their little jaunt with a skip. Her other-worldly modern shoes left tiny heel prints, proof of the girls' existence right here and now. Em wondered at how others might view her shoes, but ultimately didn't care. They were her favorite pair: burgundy suede with a little height in the heel and originally with leather bows on the top front, one on each shoe. She had rarely asked her grandparents for anything, but she had begged for these shoes that were so modern and made her feel like a lady— and had received them for her fifteenth birthday. She had woken up in this era with the clothes on her back and, oddly, next to her pillow, these peep toe wedges. She wasn't about to part with them.

Past the field, where the hard-packed clay road headed east, there were buildings and a sense of activity: downtown. And further east from there was the big city, buried under a blanket of black polluted clouds from the steamboats on the Mississippi. Em pulled her friend this way, following her intuition. May wasn't the only one who sensed things. Emily was going to find out about her family today.

As they approached town, May tried to get her bearings. A few of the buildings and streets looked familiar, like the town she'd grown up in, but more rustic . . . and, oddly, newer. Buildings were more sparse and there were no traffic lights or motor cars whizzing by. The main streets were paved and relatively well-kept, filled with carriages and wagons pulled by horses and mules.

"We should have asked Row what year—" May started, but was interrupted by a high-pitched squeal and a terrible thud. The girls whirled around to see a black woman shielding a baby, while a huge white man towered over her ominously, shaking a beefy fist at her. They were in front of a wagon being driven by a slave man, who didn't make a move to defend the lady who was crumpled in a heap on the earth. May instinctively wanted to run the other direction, but Em just as instinctively ran toward the uproar, dragging May with her.

As they approached, they heard the woman in a calm and measured voice, reasoning with the lug as if she were debating a trivial social issue at a cocktail party. "Sir, I have here Master Shelby Jackson's grand-baby. I only brought him to town to see a doctor."

"Neither of you has a right to be riding in a carriage and you don't have any papers! How do I know you're not a liar?" He stomped a threatening boot down next to the woman's hand.

"Because they're with us!"

May looked around to see who had spoken up and was panicked to realize it was Emily. Em stepped forward, staring the man down as if he were an overgrown pest at an elementary school. "Shelby

Jackson sent us . . . to get care for his grandchild." She lied as smoothly as she could considering she knew nothing about the words coming out of her mouth.

"Well, let's see your pass, girl." The thug turned his attention toward Emily. May's heart expanded with every erratic heartbeat until it felt like it would choke her right there on the spot.

As he came toward Em and May, Em suddenly screamed, "Run!" and May wholeheartedly obeyed. They darted away from the man, bumping into some onlookers and headed for an alleyway. As they turned, May saw that the woman on the ground had taken the opportunity to also run in the opposite direction. Their pursuer, easily winded, paused to decide which party he should chase. He slowed enough to give the girls a lead in this unfamiliar territory, but they didn't stop running.

The bitingly chilly air which before had felt so unwelcome was now just what May needed after running for her life, battling cumbersome petticoats and a heavy long skirt. A glimmer of sweat emerged on her forehead along her hairline. At the backside of a church and out of sight, May and Em finally collapsed against the painted clapboard wall, below a window. May heard Em gasping and panting and presumably starting to sob. Only when May looked over at Em, she wasn't crying at all, she was laughing. May wondered if her friend had completely lost her mind.

6

War and Peace

May felt guilty for it, but she was scared. She wanted to feel brave; she wanted to feel like Em appeared to—totally liberated and ready for adventure. For all May's talk of romance and excitement, she had nothing to show for it in this moment. But the sight of the colored woman on the ground being treated like a stray dog had made her sick to her stomach. The fact that Em had stepped up to help while May had just stood there quivering didn't make her feel any better.

May leaned her head back against the wall of the church and closed her eyes to shut out her surroundings. She took deep gulping breaths of icy cool air, felt it fill her lungs, and let it sting her nostrils on the way back out. Her heartbeat started to recover from its rapid rate, but not for long.

"There they are! They said they were related to Shelby Jackson —" Em pointed excitedly past a berm behind the church where the carriage they had seen earlier plodded along a road heading south of town.

May wanted to correct her friend—they weren't related to Shelby Jackson, they were owned by him. But May didn't have the energy to point out with any sense of delicacy that Em's long-lost ancestors appeared to be slave owners. "I'm not sure this is a good idea, Em," was all May could muster instead.

"We need to go catch up with them. You said yourself you wanted me to find my relatives." Em's words weren't persuasive, but the pitiful look on her face was. May knew she was being manipulated by Em's big brown puppy dog eyes, but words were failing her, her reasoning skills weakened by a torrent of compassion for Em.

"We'd better hurry to catch up, then," May sighed.

Em grabbed her hand and they were off and running again. In just a few minutes, they'd caught up to the wagon and Em hollered for them to stop.

The woman looked more afraid of the girls than she'd been of the man about to hit her in the street. The colored driver, the same man who'd been unable to help the woman in the street earlier, said, "We don' want no trouble," and waved them away.

Thinking quickly, May said, "Mrs. Nolan—" hoping that was Row's great-grandmother's name " —sent us to see Master Shelby Jackson."

The man pulled back on the reins and the horse slowed. The man and the woman both looked the girls over with suspicion.

Then May sputtered, "Soldiers!"

Coming toward them on the road from the south were five soldiers, two on horses. In blue uniforms with long guns and little blue caps, the soldiers looked as war-torn as May was already starting to feel. Her mind raced: blue uniforms. Union or Confederate? They'd been spending a lot more time in school learning about two other more recent wars than the war fought on their own turf, the Civil War.

The man driving the carriage pulled the horse to a complete stop when he heard the fear in May's voice and saw the panic flash across her face.

"Don' worry now, they ain't bushwackers. Unless theys disguised."

"Oh, hush, Judah!" said the woman, holding the baby closer to her chest. "Climb in now. We best keep movin'." She gestured to the girls.

Em scrambled aboard and put her hand out to May. May suddenly felt more uncoordinated than usual and couldn't get her foot up high enough on the carriage step. Her layers of skirting didn't help. Em saw how flustered May was and whispered, "It's OK."

May glanced gratefully at Em and her boot found purchase. The woman and Em pulled her into the carriage just as the soldiers met with them on the road.

One of the soldiers on horseback had a handlebar mustache and rotting teeth. It took all of May's might to not cover her nose with her hand in reaction to the pungent smell of the soldiers and their horses.

The man saluted Judah, but with an air of derision. He then addressed Judah with a derogatory name that made May's skin crawl. May wondered how a Union soldier, supposedly fighting for the emancipation of slaves, could speak with such disrespect. "Where ya taking the white girls?" the soldier barked.

"They goin' with us to—" the woman started.

"Didn't ask you. You always speak outta turn, girl?" The soldier spat a fountain of greasy-looking spittle from the side of his mouth. *That explains his disgusting teeth*, thought May with a shudder.

"Yessuh, sorry, sir," Judah apologized. "We's takin' the girls a' Master Shelby Jackson."

Two of the soldiers on foot shook their heads and laughed bitterly. "You mean that coward Crawford Dunkelman's daddy-in-law? Be amazed if them two men make it through this war without bein' hanged."

"That's enough," the soldier on the chestnut colored horse snapped. To the carriage full of passengers, he said, "Be on yer way. And look out fer bushwackers. About thirty of 'em came through here two days ago."

"Yessuh, thankin' you kindly fer th' warnin," Judah said. He lost no time in urging the horse and carriage forward.

As they lurched along, May and Em gazed at each other. Em's glassy eyed enthusiasm remained, but May's stomach had dropped out.

"Is this Shelby Jackson's grand-baby?" Em said, scooting closer to the woman. She put her hand toward the baby, but the woman swiped it away.

"He ain't well," the woman said. After glancing at Em, she seemed to soften. "My apologies. I'm havin' a hard time gettin' help fer li'l Noah."

Em gasped and clamped her hand over her mouth and she shot a look at May, whose eyes widened. "This *is* Noah?"

Now the woman pulled the blanket away for Em and May to see. The baby looked like an oversized wrinkled bean with a mess of fine black hair. His face glistened with sweat and he appeared feverish. His little eyes were clamped shut as if concentrating on trying to find sleep.

"Yes," the woman said. "I'm Eliza, that's Judah, and this here our boy, Noah."

It took a moment before Em pried her gaze from the baby and looked up to Eliza. "I thought you said this was Shelby Jackson's grandson?"

"Oh, he is that," Eliza said and wrapped the baby back up and hugged him tight. "Because Shelby Jackson's my daddy."

Judah barked a reprimand at Eliza for her public admission, reminding her that more importantly, she was Master Jackson's property.

Em stared at the floorboards of the wagon in a stunned silence. Not only were her ancestors slave owners, they were slaves. She had known nothing of her heritage, but she'd never thought to imagine that she was anything other than white.

❖　　❖　　❖

Back at Row's house —the Nolans' farm —that night at bedtime, May's stomach rumbled with hunger, but she had been too out of sorts to eat all day. She could barely keep straight the order of events since morning, but the events themselves were seared into her memory as if they were happening over and over again, right on top of each other.

May had learned a little more about the Jackson family and their slaves. Shelby's wife was the ill-reputed, spoiled, and abusive Willimina. Their daughter, Daisy, had married Crawford Dunkelman.

Jackson Family Tree

Eva (slave) + Master Shelby Jackson

Eliza (b. 1839. Marries Judah)

Noah (b. 1861. Marries Emilia 1888)

Judah (named for Noah's father; b. 1890. Marries Roberta Wallace. Has 3 sons)

Jeremiah (b. 1910 marries Lillian Parks)
(both d. 1931)

Emily (b. 1930)

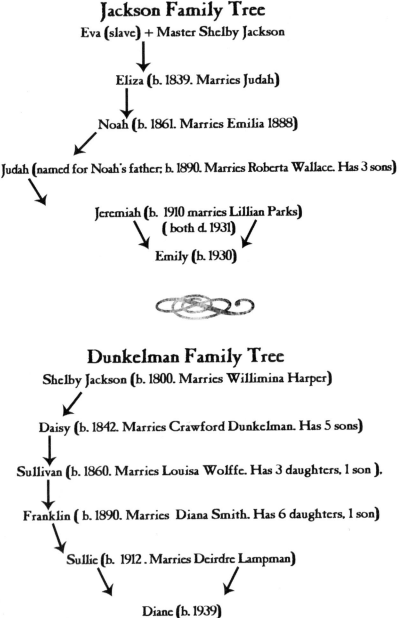

Dunkelman Family Tree

Shelby Jackson (b. 1800. Marries Willimina Harper)

Daisy (b. 1842. Marries Crawford Dunkelman. Has 5 sons)

Sullivan (b. 1860. Marries Louisa Wolffe. Has 3 daughters, 1 son).

Franklin (b. 1890. Marries Diana Smith. Has 6 daughters, 1 son)

Sullie (b. 1912 . Marries Deirdre Lampman)

Diane (b. 1939)
Franco (b. 1944)

Because the white-haired, white-skinned Shelby Jackson had more than 20 slaves, his estate was officially considered a plantation; his son-in-law Crawford, whose property bordered the Jacksons', had five slaves, relegating Crawford's estate to a mere farm. Though the two masters' homes were near each other, so that Willimina and Daisy could visit without a lot of fuss, the slaves' quarters were at opposite corners of the grounds, making it difficult for families and friends to connect anywhere other than work, where there was no time or occasion for socializing.

Emily's great-great-grandmother, Eliza Jackson, used to be Willimina's slave, May learned. But Eliza was the daughter of Eva—a slave woman—and Shelby. Willimina was a strong woman whom poison couldn't kill, but she claimed that the presence of Eliza made her ill; she said the girl had a contagious sickness, or demons, or an aura, that was tormenting Willimina. Maybe what tormented Willimina was the fact that Eliza had Willimina's husband's eyes. And so Eliza was "gifted" to Daisy and in Eliza's place, Shelby bought a slave named Virginia "Gin" Harrison from a cotton plantation in Louisiana that was struggling to stay afloat.

This was all information that took May several conversations over subsequent days to absorb. But that first morning that May and Emily had fought their way onto Judah and Eliza's wagon, Eliza had brought the girls to Gin's kitchen at Willimina's house. It was obvious Eliza didn't know what else to do with them. Gin was a whirlwind of orderly activity. She seemed to be fixing a tea tray, cleaning beans, and mending Master Shelby's pants and scrubbing mud off his boots all at the same time. Eliza and Gin didn't greet each other; they seemed to start right where they left off. It reminded May of herself and Row and Em. But the sweet connection she had with her friends was where the comparisons ended. Seeing Gin's beauty, strength, and the haunted look in her eyes made May's heart break in the way it had when she'd learned about Row's mom passing away. May selfishly hoped she would never understand first-hand how someone could continue to function in the face of such adversity.

"Doctor?" Gin asked after Noah simply, tending to her duties without acknowledging May and Em.

Eliza shook her head no and went to work with one hand on the beans without being asked, holding the baby with the other.

"You'll be wantin' me to work some magic with Master Shelby, then, to get the baby some help?"

"Lawd willin', he listen to you," Eliza said in a pleading tone, keeping her voice low.

May and Em looked around the kitchen. There were none of the modern conveniences of a 1945 kitchen: no electrified toaster, no coffee percolator, no washer with a wringer, and certainly no mobile dishwasher like the one Row's mother had installed. Of course, there was no radio sitting in the corner waiting to fill the home with Glenn Miller or soap operas. May was surprised to note that the floor was a glossy linoleum, much like her mother's kitchen floor. Only the colors were different and this floor less worn than hers. The over-sized oven along one wall wheezed gently, a bucket of coal nearby. Though it looked practically medieval, May had a feeling it was an expensive and "modern" amenity. The day outside was chilly, but inside this small room, the air was hot and stifling, the pungent yeasty smell of baking bread rich and overwhelming.

May noticed that Gin carried herself with a quiet confidence that was missing from Eliza's demeanor.

"The girls?" Gin asked, her first recognition of the visitors.

"Here to see Master Shelby," Eliza said.

"We're . . . orphans," faltered May, praying silently for forgiveness from her parents.

The excitement and wonder that had animated Em's face earlier was long gone and she gaped at May with desperate, pleading eyes. May's head began to throb, a side effect of the guilt wracking her heart. This was her fault.

"We're here with a message from the Nolan family." May tried to think fast. "But we don't have to see Master Shelby. You can give him the message."

Emily squeezed May's hand hopefully, waiting for a response.

"What message?" Gin had moved to an adjoining room, filled with canned and dried goods and stacks of plates—the butler's pantry.

"The . . . uh, the Nolans offered to help little Noah." May regretted the words as they tumbled out of her mouth. What was she doing? Her urgent need to be back with Row had forged this terrible lie. Maybe it would at least get her and Em back with Row, but what about poor little Noah?

"Who the Nolans? He a doctor?" Eliza asked, rocking the baby hopefully.

Gin looked carefully at May as she emerged from the pantry. "I think I know them Nolans. Irish. He ain't no doctor." She added in a whisper, "Ain't they abolitionists?"

"I don't know, ma'am. I just know that she . . . ." May cleared her throat, felt the oppressive heat of the room threaten to drop her like a dollop of melted butter on the kitchen floor. "She's good at nursing children; babies, especially."

Gin was suddenly serious and intense. She stepped up to May, focusing on her as if she were trying to see into her very soul. Though they were almost the same height, and Gin only a year or two older,

Gin seemed to tower over May. "You listen. I don' know how Nolans know about a sick baby all the way out here at Master Shelby's, but you girls talking life and death. Mrs. Willimina fin' out that baby getting special attention over other slave chillun and Eliza will get beat ta death, hear?" She turned to Eliza, pointing her finger forcefully. "You go now. An' fix the baby. I can't make no excuses for you after this afternoon." Though Gin was years younger than Eliza, Eliza accepted Gin's directives without hesitation.

"But, Judah has to take us," Eliza squeaked.

Gin again ducked into the pantry and came back out. "Then, the story is, he takin' you to get me flour. 'Sides, you need to bring somethin' to Mrs. Nolan as a payment, so you will be needin' flour after you bring this to 'er." She heaved a ten pound sack of flour between Em and May and they caught it before it sank to the floor in a heavy thud. "Better not be seen with that headin' out," she advised, cautioning them against getting caught for stealing it.

Then Gin turned back to her work as if she had never been interrupted.

❖ ❖ ❖

Wednesday, November 14, 1864!

Dear Diary,

You are a witness. I woke up this morning to a new world...no, an old, old world. My house hasn't even been built yet, my parents haven't been born...the watch is most certainly to blame for all of this.

I cannot sleep tonight and could not eat. Row and I are at her house and I'm horrified to say that I don't know for sure where Emily is. The last time I saw her, we had just discovered that her great-grandfather was the grandchild of a slave and a slave master. Which means Emily is part colored. I've never had a colored friend before. But...that's not true! I've been friends with Em all this time. She must feel different. But I feel the same about her; she's still Em. And, oh, I _do_ love her dearly.

Diary, I haven't stopped lying since we got here! Everyone thinks we are orphans of the war and are hiring us out to work in exchange for food and a place to stay. In trying to get help for Baby Noah (Emily's great grandfather!!), I said that Row's great-grandma could nurse the baby back to health. I suggested it because she had a baby herself...but mainly because I wanted to find a way for Em, me and even Noah to get off the horrible estate full of slaves and cruel people who treat them like dirt. I wanted Em and me to be at Row's house with Row where we could use the watch somehow to get back home. Funny how I thought leaving home was an escape and now I want nothing more than to go home.

On our way off the plantation, Crawford Dunkelman stopped us and dragged Eliza off the wagon. He asked which one of us was the orphan he ordered (as if he can order people up like items out of Sears Roebuck catalog!) Before I could even open my mouth, Emily volunteered herself. I could see she was worried for Eliza. Dunkelman whipped the horse to get Judah and me out of his sight and to take the baby for help. I'm scared that he treats his horses no worse than the people he holds captive to work for him. He was so awful; I will never forget those eyes. It was a combination of intelligence (like he knew exactly what he was doing) and cruelty (but he didn't care). I sobbed all the way to the Nolans', holding the sick baby and trying not to get him wet with my tears. I know I should have been stronger, should have kept myself from crying so, but I couldn't. I should have spoken up and offered to stay with Emily, too. I am a coward and the worst friend.

Judah told me that the plantation was suffering financially from the war and many slaves would soon be sold off, separated from their families. New Year's Day slaves are bought and sold with no say in staying or going. He knew he didn't have long with his own family Eliza, Noah and a little girl named Violet.

I suppose I guessed right because Mrs. Fiona did help Noah. At least I saw some compassion and bravery today in the face of the sickening inhumanity that is an open wound on this country's countenance. I know first hand what people in this country did to each other and I can't un-know it. Right "now" President Lincoln is still alive; he has already made the Emancipation Proclamation, but because there is a war over what Lincoln wants, most slaves are still not free. Of course, I know that the war ends and the slaves are freed, but I don't know what ultimately happens to these kind and wonderful people that I've met, Emily's family and Miss Gin.

I've never seen someone like Gin before. She bears

the brunt of this war, but she takes care of people like me, a white stranger, and has a hope in her eyes that makes me want to cry. I wish I could stop all this; but I can't. Even if we make it home, I can't stop what history did. I can only be inspired by Gin's strength and loveliness, Emily's bravery, Judah's and the Nolans' kindness. Signing off to pray now before I hold this watch to my heart and try to get us home.

Marion G. Boggs

I KNOW LIFE AFTER MOM, AFTER MY BROTHERS, DURING WAR. NOW I KNOW LIFE BEFORE MOM, BEFORE MY BROTHERS, BEFORE MY WHOLE FAMILY. I'M A STRANGER IN MY OWN LIFE, LIVING THROUGH A DIFFERENT WAR.
AS MUCH AS I HATE WAR, I SEE NOW MORE THAN EVER WHY THEY MUST BE FOUGHT. WE CAN NEVER TOLERATE HATRED AND IGNORANCE THAT BINDS PEOPLE – CAN NEVER STAND BY AND LET IT HAPPEN. IF WE AREN'T FIGHTING AGAINST IT, WE ARE SUPPORTING IT.
GOD BLESS THE SOLDIERS WHO SACRIFICE THEMSELVES FOR PEOPLE THEY WILL NEVER KNOW. WE ALL MUST BE SOLDIERS. AND I MUST FIGHT, LIKE MY FAMILY, FOR WHAT IS RIGHT
– ROWENA
SAT. 11-12-1864 ???

Dear Diary,   Sat. Nov. 12, 1864

This may be the last entry into my diary. In fact, this is written on stationery and with a quill, both of which I stole from Willimina Shelby's study at the Big House (yes, I am a thief now . . . and so much more). I will have to add this page to my diary if I ever see my diary again. Earlier today I never guessed I would feel like I do now. I feel like. . . like, well . . . I am <u>home</u>. Oh, it's not a happy home, or happy place (certainly I would never consider a plantation <u>my home</u>). But for the first time in my life, I know where I came from and in a strange way, the future opens up to me. All my life, I just assumed I was white. Row's family is Irish, Marion's is German. I just thought I was some mixture that was too varied to identify and take pride in. Now I know that my ancestors were slaves and slave owners. I would rather be colored descendant of slaves than the granddaughter of a wealthy slave master any day of any year. Unfortunately, I am both.

I heard Mrs. Willimina say that God made slavery for the white man to be productive. But I know that around here, most of the slaves pray and sing to God for deliverance from slavery. I asked Gin, how come if there's one God, He could tell two people two different things? She said, "I guess one of 'em don't hear so good."

Oh! Gin has just seen me writing and wants me to teach her how, even though it is midnight and she must be exhausted. I will have to tell my story later, for now I must try, in some small way, to repay Gin and Eliza for what they have done for me and my family.

Did my parents and do my grandparents know the truth about us?

       ~Emily

7

Yours Truly, Anonymous

Marion Boggs Fairview could imagine what Maxine Marshall was going through. It was Maxine's right to speak up, of course, and besides that, she had felt protected by anonymity to write things that she would never speak aloud. Maxine's article in *The Invisible Truth* had come out last Thursday and had gone largely unnoticed. It only took the big mouth of one popular girl, who was paranoid about becoming forgotten, to make a drama—a mockery—of Maxine's essay. Diane Dunkelman.

"Why am I in trouble?" Diane pouted, twirling her hair around her finger.

"I keep telling you, no one's in trouble. I just wanted to get the two of you together before things get out of hand," Mrs. Fairview said. Out in the hallway of Mrs. F's classroom, it was even noisier than usual. Not only was it after school, it was nearing the end of the school year. It was as if the rules of the school year were wearing thin and could no longer bear the weight of the season. The two girls sat in desks in front of the class and Mrs. F leaned against her own desk. She tried to be impartial as she looked between fair-haired, spoiled Diane and dark-complected, thoughtful Maxine, whose expressive brown eyes were cast down as they had been all day. Mrs. F wanted to scream and make Diane apologize, but it wasn't her battle to fight. Or was it? The rush of memories, images of people she once knew, crowded her thought, almost incapacitating her ability to think straight.

Long-lost Emily Jackson. Gin Harris.

Mrs. F felt something catch in her throat and urged herself to focus on the situation directly at hand.

"Well, I guess if she apologizes now, it won't be as bad," said Diane. She began to pull her cell phone out of her pocket, no doubt to text someone as she constantly did in Mrs. F's third period current events class.

With a swift motion, Mrs. F confiscated Diane's metal appendage and assured Diane she would get it back after their meeting. Mrs. F took two deep breaths, one after the other, to keep her blood from boiling. She was far from objective in this situation, for so many reasons. In as even a tone as she could muster, she asked Diane, "What is it you believe Maxine should apologize for?"

Maxine kept her eyes averted, but her jaw tightened. Diane seemed to have lost interest in the incident without an audience. She answered lamely, "For the mean things she said about white people." She sighed dramatically, and recited from memory, "*Until Whites stop living as if they set the standard for normal and everyone of color is abnormal, this generation and all the others following it will be useless.*"

Now Maxine looked up sharply, her brows furrowed in puzzlement. She wondered, first of all, at Diane's having memorized even part of Maxine's essay, and secondly, at what exactly Diane found so offensive about the statement she quoted. Why had Diane not quoted the line immediately following, *And until we embrace the best of ourselves that our past has caused us to be, we can never have the humility to let go of our mistakes and accept our glorious future?* Mrs. F made a reassuring, slight gesture with her hand in Maxine's direction. Her gold watch caught a sparkle of light and glittered. Maxine remained quiet as Mrs. F asked as calmly as she could, "What makes that statement mean?"

"Just because you play favorites, don't act all clueless about what Maxine wrote in that stupid paper." Diane made a big play of rolling her eyes and shaking her head so that her hair fell around her shoulders in golden, mesmerizing ripples.

"I don't appreciate the tone, Diane," Mrs. F said. "I also don't appreciate when students spread rumors—"

"—which is exactly what she did!" Diane interrupted, jabbing her finger accusingly at Maxine.

Now Maxine's mouth flew open. First in shock, then to unleash a torrent of words. "I didn't write anything that was untrue! I wasn't mean, I didn't call anyone names, which is more than I can say for *some* people—"

Though Mrs. F would have liked to hear what else Maxine had to say, she had to maintain control and try to resolve the conflict before it got worse for Maxine—and Maxine's friends. "Both of you, we are having a discussion, not a boxing match. I ask that you please respect—"

Once again, Diane cut her teacher off, storming at her, "Oh, puh-*lease*. I love how it's a *discussion*. Why am I even here? She should be suspended for hate speech and *bullying* and I should be rewarded for figuring out it was her who wrote that racist trash! When my parents hear about this, they will make sure you're fired!"

"She's retiring, you *airhead*!" yelled Maxine, jumping up from the desk, her books clattering to the floor.

"Maxine!" bellowed Mrs. F. Now Maxine had done it. If she had just kept her cool long enough . . . but how could she, with everything going on that Diane Dunkelman would never have a clue about? Mrs. F could hardly blame Maxine.

Diane's lip quivered and tears—no doubt summoned at her command for effect—shimmered in her eyes. "That . . . that's what I mean, Mrs. Fairview. She's so cruel. You can't argue with me now!" Diane's tone of voice had gone from insolent to victimized in a heartbeat.

"Diane, would you kindly *shut up*?" Mrs. F regretted it as soon as the words flew out of her mouth. She fumbled, "Please close your mouth for one minute . . . . ."

Diane gasped, "You told me to shut up; you told me to *shut up*!" Her voice was so high it was nearly a whisper. And it was so comical, Maxine had to make a big effort to keep from bursting out in laughter. But seeing the look on Mrs. F's face helped her maintain her composure. Mrs. F looked defeated. She had just added fuel to a fire she was trying to put out.

"I'm sorry, Diane," Maxine rushed to say. "I'm sorry for those awful things I wro—"

Once again, her teacher interrupted her. "No, Maxine Marshall, you are not to apologize to Diane Dunkelman. Diane, Maxine didn't do a thing wrong. What she wrote was not hate speech and it was not racist. She was not bullying anyone. She wrote from the heart about issues that affect all of us, and we'd do a lot better if we could listen and join the conversation instead of creating drama where there is no drama. I'm sorry if I offended you—"

"—when you told me to shut up?"

"—when I asked you to shut your mouth and not interrupt me. I shouldn't have said it in that way."

Now Diane looked smug. A look crossed her eyes that Mrs. F had seen before. She sucked in her breath. *Crawford Dunkelman*, all those years ago. A chill rushed through every vein in Mrs. F's body, instantly replacing the heat of anger.

"*Thanks* for your lame attempt at an apology, but I don't think this is over. For either of you. By a long shot," Diane said, rising from her desk smoothly. She held her hand out for her phone, placing her other hand on her hip and tossing her hair. Mrs. F offered the phone limply and Diane grabbed it, pushing buttons before she even looked at it. She headed for the door, but right before going through it, she wheeled around to Mrs. F and Maxine with tears streaming down her face. "Daddy?" she said into the phone, her voice weak and unsteady. "I need your help." Then, in the split second before she turned to go out the door, she flashed a wickedly cheerful smile at Mrs. F and Maxine.

❖ ❖ ❖

Judy's house seemed claustrophobic. Mary, sitting with Judy, Ann, and Bev and waiting for Maxine to arrive, wanted to be anywhere but there. No, that wasn't true. Not *anywhere*. In one fell swoop, her life had gone from dreamy to dumpy. She couldn't stand to look at lovely Ann sitting across the kitchen table from her. Ann with her dark hair, her sophisticated and hep clothes, her timeless Princess Grace beauty. Who could blame James for thinking she was deep and appealing—what had he written in that poem?—*deeper waters leave no trail*. It didn't take jets to figure out that James O'Grady liked Ann. Of course, if he had in fact written the poem, Mary could figure that he liked Mary just as much if she was supposed to be the "temperamental" one with "sunset-colored hair." The thought of that first real conversation she'd had with James, at sunset in the park, made her heart sink like a heavy stone into her stomach. Her fun afternoon with the girls and James at a diner over the weekend was now meaningless. If James didn't know if he liked Ann or Mary more, than Mary was happy—no, *thrilled*—to give him up. She wouldn't make the same mistakes her mother had in falling for a guy who couldn't make up his mind. James was a creep, and she would tell herself that as often as she needed to.

But every time she thought it, she wanted to cry. It was obvious that she wasn't the only one on edge.

Judy said, "Do you think Maxine likes us even though we're white? She wrote here, *White is not normal, it is only the lack of pigment in someone's skin. But Black is more than not abnormal, it is the pigment of an oppressed population.*" Judy read from *The Invisible Truth* even though she knew that line by heart.

"Speaking of white, why is everything black or white with you, Judy?" Bev said.

"What do you mean?" Judy sensed the unusually irritated tone in Bev's voice.

"I mean . . . why do we have to decide if Maxine likes us or not, or what she meant by what she wrote? *If* she wrote it—"

Judy, Ann, and Mary all made soft indignant sounds.

"—OK, she wrote it. But don't you think that the fact she's *our friend* means she likes us?"

"It's hard to tell *what* people really think. They can say one thing, but mean another," said Mary crossly, although she actually didn't think Maxine had written anything offensive.

"Who put the salt in your coffee?" Bev said.

"Leave her alone," Ann said gently. She had a feeling she knew what this was about with Mary. The poem that was printed in the same paper as Maxine's essay, the poem that was probably written by James O'Grady . . . and probably written about her and Mary. The poem that had helped her get over James. But Mary wasn't having as easy a go at it as Ann had. Ann had memorized the poem and did not doubt that its words were just as familiar to Mary:

"sunset-colored hair,
and temper's flare
boating hat without a sail,
deeper currents leave no trail
. . . passion?
. . . or security?
love's forever question."

Bev protested to Ann, "Hey, why am I getting picked on? You were—" Before she could say something she'd regret, Bev was interrupted by a knock at the front door.

Ann rushed to answer it, while the others sat unmoving at the kitchen table. Ann opened the door to Maxine, immediately taking her hand and clutching it as she led her inside and out of the heat of the blistering late May day. She had half a mind to tell Maxine to run in the other direction, but instead just held her hand until they got into the kitchen and gave it one last squeeze before dropping it.

Maxine, usually alert and attentive, even if she wasn't always vocal, looked drained and tired. Judy seemed not to notice and launched right in. "As you can probably guess, this meeting is to discuss what you wrote—"

"This is a meeting? Oh, swell," sighed Maxine, slumping into a seat at the end of the table. It hadn't even occurred to her that her friends would find reason to take offense. She was still reeling from her sister's harangue; and she hadn't even begun to deal with what had just happened at school with Mrs. Fairview and Diane Dunkelman.

"Well, we are interested in what you think about us," Judy said and instantly regretted how it sounded.

Suddenly, Maxine's eyes blazed to life. "Tell me exactly what this is about." She leaned forward and Judy found herself sitting back.

"Aw, Maxine, it's not about anything," Bev asserted. Not so much as peacemaker as conflict-avoider.

"Don't put words in my mouth!" Judy said to Bev. "It's about that essay you wrote. We—"

"Speak for yourself," muttered Bev under her breath.

"We," Judy emphasized, "Want to know if . . . if . . . if you have a problem with us—"

Maxine stared at her.

"—with us being . . . *white*." Judy finished with less confidence than she'd started with. Now that she had said it out loud to her friend's face, she felt foolish. She wished she could start the conversation over. She looked up to Maxine, trusted her. Loved her. But she hated feeling stupid and didn't understand Maxine's essay or the indignant tone with which it was written. Besides that, she'd never really known a colored—or, as people were saying nowadays, *Black*—person before. It just wasn't done in her world in the fifties. When Maxine had come over for the slumber party at Judy's house, Bitsy had warned Judy to go carefully. "Having a colored friend won't do you any favors with the world at large," Bitsy had said. Judy had initially tried to pass over the comment; she was disappointed in her mother for saying it. Now Judy felt like she was beyond questioning her relationship with Maxine; Maxine was more than a colored girl —she was Judy's friend.

"My problem," Maxine said slowly, rising from the table in slow motion, "isn't with you—or anyone—being white. It's with ignorance. Did you know that the first slumber party you had, I had to go without washing my hair for two weeks because I missed beauty parlor at my friend Nan's house that night? Did you know that I've put myself in danger hanging out with white girls? Did you realize that we got kicked out of the library that first week in 1955 not because we were loud but because I'm Negro? White people don't like seeing me around you, but there are some folks in *my* church and *my* neighborhood who don't like it either. Not just because of what they think I might do to you, but because you might hurt me. Because of situations just like this. No, people don't know the first thing about me, because they don't ask. They just assume. They sit in their *ivory towers*, concerned only with themselves. Next time you don't know something, Judy, just ask."

Judy frowned. *Hadn't* she just asked?

Maxine didn't pause. "Now if you'll excuse me, I need to go home and brace my parents for the fact that I may have just gotten suspended from school."

Ann and Bev gasped. "Oh, no!" said Ann. She reached out her hand to Maxine, but Maxine didn't take it; instead, she whirled around, her penny loafers making a squeak against Judy's mother's tiled kitchen floor. And before anyone could ask her for details, Maxine had marched herself to the front door, let herself out, and slammed the door decisively behind her. Oh, she knew she was being dramatic—maybe even more dramatic than Judy, if that was possible.

But how could her friends—people that claimed to be her friends—take what she had written personally? How could they not see what she saw—that she was treated differently than they were, that just because they had a president of color now didn't mean everything was peachy keen? They were so wrapped up in their own worlds. They had this grand adventure together, but it wasn't about being together, it was about getting back home. Once they were home, she wondered, would they be friends? Or would they have used each other to get want they wanted?

Maxine thought of everything the Fifties Chix didn't know about her and wondered if they could truly be considered friends. They didn't know what it was like for her to walk into a predominantly white school every morning. They didn't know how she tortured herself to have presentable hair . . . the chemicals, the burning, the heavy grease. Maxine hated thinking about things as petty as her hair, but still, it was a fact of life.

She wasn't looking where she was going, she was so absorbed in her thoughts. James's blue rattletrap car rolled up next to her.

"Hey!" James called out cheerfully.

Maxine gave him a half-hearted wave.

"I'm looking for Mary. Seen her?"

"She's at Judy's," Maxine said distractedly.

"Well, thanks—um, are you OK?"

Still walking as his car rolled slowly beside her, Maxine found herself shaking her head no.

"Hop in," James invited. "It's too hot to walk, anyway." He pulled the car to a stop and waited. She kept walking, then she too stopped. She paused a moment and then went back a few steps and crossed to his car after seeing no one else around. He pushed the passenger side door open. She plopped in, staring straight ahead. All she could think was how she was sitting in a white boy's car. This never would have happened in 1955 without serious consequences. But James didn't seem concerned, didn't seem to care who noticed.

It was silent for a whole minute. Finally James said, "So . . . ?"

That one little syllable opened a floodgate and Maxine unleashed her thoughts. She barely took a breath, telling him about her sister, her meeting with Mrs. F and Diane, and even about the "meeting" with her friends. Then she told him, not caring that the math didn't add up, about her great-grandmother Gin being a slave. Maybe it wasn't something she should have spoken out loud, in mixed company and especially sitting alone with him in a car where everyone could see, but he didn't recoil or make a sympathetic clicking sound, he just listened. In fact, he didn't say a word through her entire diatribe.

After several minutes, she was done. James just nodded his head. He didn't offer advice or ask clarifying questions. Maxine was relieved. After a moment or two of silence, he pulled the car away from the curb and headed for her house.

Still, he didn't speak, but they both felt comfortable in the silence. He parked in her driveway and she thanked him for the ride, glancing around, still scared about the repercussions of being seen in a white boy's car. But no neighbors were visible, so she let herself breathe just for a moment.

"I love quotes," James said, right before Maxine was going to close the car door. It seemed a non sequitur, but she paused to listen since it was the first time he'd said anything. "There's a quote from some famous writer or artist or musician or politician for every occasion. You know which one fits right now? Our president said, 'I miss being anonymous.'"

For the first time all day, Maxine found herself smiling. "Yeah. Me, too."

8

Trading Off

May Boggs was exhausted, but that was the least of her problems. After Row's great-grandmother Fiona had given the baby Noah some mysterious "Irish remedy" that resembled hot butter and liquor and had passed him back to Judah, Judah had left without May in a hurry. Her stomach churned with acidic worry as she watched him drive the wagon away toward her friend trapped on a plantation in wretched conditions with a wild-eyed, unpredictable slave master.

After she and Row had cleaned the kitchen after supper (a much different prospect than at home or in Row's modern 1940s kitchen), they took their sewing into the parlor and sat by the fire. Every bone in May's body ached; she'd run, walked, cleaned, worried, lied, and labored more in one day than in her entire lifetime before. Yet she was no closer to getting the three of them back to 1945. She wished she could just curl up on her mother's red velvet settee and listen to Glenn Miller, Nat King Cole, or Bing Crosby; or sneak off to the cinema with Row and Em to see the latest musical and footage of the post-war victory parades.

Simply connecting with Row privately to review all the facts and events of the day—as bizarre as it was that the day was in 1864—was complicated, as the Nolans, Fiona, and Fiona's husband, Lachlan, were also sitting by the fire, talking over the events of their day. Lachlan Nolan—Row's great-grandfather—turned out to be the tall lanky redhead they'd seen on the wagon outside when the girls had first woken up that morning. He'd been working outside until supper and now reclined, tipped back on a wooden chair while he read the Bible, literature, and poetry, mostly out loud. Lachlan's brogue was at once comforting and entertaining as he read every passage with expression. Fiona kept swiping at him with her knitting to put all four legs of the chair on the floor, but he disregarded her with a twinkle in his eye. They each nursed a small ceramic cup of aromatic tea. Fiona told her husband how Judah came to bring a baby to their house for care. It was clear from their conversation that they were abolitionists and loyal to the North, though they would never say so openly outside their own home, even though Missouri was technically a Union state. They probably would have directly taken in and sheltered Noah, Judah, and the whole slave family, if the penalty wasn't death. But May could tell from their conversation that they hadn't ruled out helping and she made note of it.

Row marveled at how relaxed the couple seemed, considering their circumstances and what she knew from researching her family tree. Lachlan had served the Union army the first two years of the war, and he and Fiona would eventually have five children and twelve grandchildren—one of whom would be Row's dad, Walter Nolan. Row couldn't have imagined there was a moment in their day for leisure or a selfish thought. She had been at Fiona's side helping grind flour (unfortunately, Judah had brought a sack of flour just after she and Fiona had ground their own), gather eggs (and then slaughter one of the chickens), cure pork meat, do wash, muck out the horse stall, feed the pigs, mend woolen mittens, and prepare three meals —all while caring for the baby. It boggled her mind that this process would be repeated over and over every day . . . and that eventually, four more babies would be added to the mix.

On top of the daily grind was the threat of war. Not the kind of war her brothers had gone to fight in another land, but battles that could be heard booming at noon just miles away and soldiers begging for either help or food at the front door, or being caught at the back door trying to steal chickens or other food and supplies that the Army wasn't providing. Regiments of soldiers marched past the house at random times night and day, announced by fife and drum, the pounding of hooves, and the clatter of their weapons. The only constant that Row could see was the tedious labor required to survive day after day. She had been here only fourteen hours, but it felt like forever. Row's feet and hands were blistered and tender, unlike Fiona's calloused hands. She dreaded staying, but equally dreading leaving, imagining all the work her great-grandmother would be left to do alone.

And Row didn't want to have to say goodbye to another family member.

So that evening, seeing the pitiful and imploring look in May's eyes drove Row to indignation and impatience. What was Row supposed to do? She was as sorry as anyone for their circumstances— particularly for Em's—but she didn't much have the option of walking away to go get a soda, or sitting out on the porch yukking it up with a high school boy or two. She couldn't even escape to her bedroom to kick up her feet and giggle and share whispered secrets, or bury her feelings in her diary. And she hadn't allowed herself the pleasure of sitting down at the upright piano to compose a new tune since her mother had passed. This was her new reality, and the feeling that this was all a dream was permanently dashed when Fiona had snapped the neck of that chicken and directed Row to pluck its feathers . . . once it stopped moving. Row had decided then and there, in that all-too-real moment, that she would never eat chicken again (a luxury during her day, anyway); but by the time supper had come, she was famished and gobbled up the chicken, biscuits, and gravy with only a fleeting sense of regret. In fact, when, at the dinner table, Lachlan had mentioned he couldn't wait until spring so they could eat fresh robin, Row hadn't had the energy to be horrified even about that.

The sun had long set, but Fiona realized the night was getting on. "Don'tcha have somewhere to be?" she asked pointedly to May.

Though Row was annoyed with her friend, she certainly didn't want May to leave. She quickly spoke up. "She doesn't have anywhere else to be."

"You also orphaned by the war?" Lachlan asked, making the same assumption about Row and May. He shook his head sympathetically.

"Yessir," May answered quietly. She'd had enough of lying for one day, but didn't know how else she could muster a bed for herself for the night.

Talk of the war sparked something in Lachlan.

"I was at Camp Jackson," he said in a confessional tone. No one else spoke, so after a moment he continued. The girls listened with goosebumps prickling up and down their flesh as Lachlan detailed the Union's raid on a Confederate camp in a park in downtown St.

Louis. The day before the raid, Captain Nathaniel Lyon had disguised himself as a woman and infiltrated the camp, noting the arsenal that was no doubt intended to be used against the Union's interest. Lyon had decided to raid the next day.

The raid and surrender had been carried out peacefully. However, leaving the camp with 650 prisoners of war in tow, Lyon's 5,000 troops had encountered spectators in the streets, who began to throw rocks and debris at the Union soldiers. Lachlan's eyes misted as he described the riot that followed, Union soldiers firing shots into the crowd and killing sixty civilians. That event served to prove Missouri's loyalty to the North as a Union state (the only slave state in the Union), but it also swiftly divided the loyalty of the residents of Missouri. Those who were called "Secesh" wanted to secede from the United States and join the Southern Confederacy and fight for states' rights (including the states' rights to allow slavery), while those siding with the North clung to the objective of a united country with every human free. Many blamed the North for the massacre on the streets that day. The Missouri governor, Clairborne Fox Jackson, had wanted Missouri to secede from the Union or stay neutral. May and Row were surprised to learn that Governor Jackson was a cousin of Shelby Jackson.

Of the massacre at Camp Jackson, on the streets of St. Louis, Lachlan explained with a catch in his voice, "We were young, untested soldiers. Many were Dutch and German and did not speak English. It was too chaotic to set it right . . . . " As his voice trailed off, Fiona reached her hand out to her husband, but this time not to chide him.

To the girls, mostly May, she said quietly, "You have a place for tonight, child, but I will be needin' your help in return come daybreak."

The girls quickly excused themselves to Row's bedroom. They were both exhausted, but still May wanted to tell Row about her day and the conditions under which she had left Em. Row was uncharacteristically snippy with May, but May forged on.

"If we leave her there, she could be sold down river," May cried.

"I don't know what to do," Row admitted in a rare display of vulnerability. "We can't leave her there, of course. But what about my family and baby Jacob? How do we save everyone?"

May's skin once again rose in frightened prickles all over her body. She sucked her breath in involuntarily. Any free thought she'd had throughout the day was consumed with the notion that they had somehow—miraculously, mysteriously, incredulously—time-traveled. Just a moment of quiet got her thoughts stirred up: What if we are not in the past at all, but in a world that coexists right along with our other world? What if we crossed over to another realm? Do Mother and Daddy know that I am missing? May thought of how panicked her mother especially would feel and her heart went out to her like never before. Oh, how she longed to be listening to the radio with her now, smelling her White Shoulders perfume and standing in the kitchen next to the sink, brushing elbows with her as they worked to prepare supper. May would tell her how much she loved her; instead of trying to escape all the time to be with her friends, she would enjoy being with her mother. Her friends didn't even have mothers, which made May a horrible ingrate . . . .

May burst into tears before she even began to contemplate missing her father. Row ran across the room to enclose her friend in a hug. "Don't worry, Marion. We'll figure this all out."

May noticed that Row hadn't said that everything would be fine, but at least she knew she wasn't alone.

❖ ❖ ❖

After a fitful sleep, Em awoke to a crying baby—her great-grand-father!—and half a dozen crowing roosters. She had slept—or rather tried to sleep—on a pallet of straw and cornhusks stuffed in a burlap bag. The ends of the straw had poked through and gouged her skin, and the burlap made her itchy. If it weren't for the dirty, oily smell of the fabric, the dank moist winter air seeping through every crack, and the total lack of privacy that came with six people living in one room, the little cabin might have seemed cozy.

Through the dim pre-dawn light, Em caught sight of the woman she now knew to be her great-grandmother soundlessly arranging a fire in a potbelly stove in the corner. The others in the room started to stir and Em took the opportunity, maybe the only quiet moment she would find all day, to study Eliza and organize her own thoughts. Em had selfishly hoped to stay with Gin at the quarters in the Jackson Plantation, ashamed to prefer Gin over her own family. Compared to Gin, Eliza seemed almost mousy. Gin had a zest for life; Eliza was resigned. Gin was confident; Eliza jumped at her own shadow. Emily hadn't understood what Gin meant the night before when she had explained to Em that Eliza hadn't wanted a baby because it was one more thing for Mrs. Willimina to hold over her head. Em thought it a terrible thing for Eliza to wish away her baby; but now, watching her arrange the wood with one hand and cradle sleeping Noah with other so tenderly, she understood that Mrs. Willimina could threaten to sell Eliza or the baby at any moment. It must have been torture for Eliza to be always scared of losing her children. Worse, Em realized, than never having them in the first place.

In a quick and quiet movement, Em was by Eliza's side. "Can I help?" she whispered and Eliza smiled, handing Em the bundle.

"He's not 'wake yet, but he needs a fresh start." It didn't take long for Em to realize that Eliza meant Noah needed to be changed. She tried to hold her breath to keep the soiled diaper smell out and maintain her composure. She had not wanted to find herself in 1864 a second day. She didn't want to abandon what she now knew was her family; but if she'd waken up in her own bed, or in a pile of soft blankets on Row's 1945 bedroom floor, she would have felt relieved.

As Em turned to clean up Noah, Eliza caught her by the arm. There was an intensity in her eyes that hadn't been there before as she spoke to Em barely louder than a breath: "I know you don' belong here."

"What do you mean?" Em's heart stopped.

"I know you think you should be workin' at the Big House with Mrs. Willimina. But, Miss Daisy here at the farm, she treat you better."

Yesterday she had been at Miss Daisy's farm, which was a vacation compared to Mrs. Willimina Jackson's plantation, where she had been sent to deliver eggs, vegetables and water from Daisy's farm. At Miss Daisy's house, Daisy checked in with her servants, making sure they were warm and fed and calling for men to do the heavy lifting; at Mrs. Willimina's house, she called the help in to chide them cruelly, make fun of the very clothing she demanded they wear, and holler at them for tardy meals (though she was the one who called them away from the duties she delegated).

For the life of her, Em couldn't reconcile how one moment, Mrs. Willimina could be having tea with her friends reverently discussing Jesus' love for all mankind, and the next moment be publicly berating the slaves whose whole lives revolved around satisfying Mrs.

Willimina's every ridiculous whim. But all the housemaids bore the verbal lashings with dignity. It was as if they had escaped to another place mentally and only their bodies stood in Mrs. Willimina's presence. This of course, enraged Mrs. Willimina even more and drove up the sharpness of her insults and shrillness of her voice.

The trade-off of the advantage of working for the kinder Miss Daisy was her cruel and conniving husband, Crawford Dunkelman; while the advantage of working for Daisy's mother, Mrs. Willimina Jackson, was Daisy's father, Shelby Jackson (Emily's great-great-grandfather, a fact she still had trouble accepting). He was fierce in his business dealings, but he strove to treat his "property" in a humane way. Miss Daisy would often sigh to her help, "I'm going to miss you when the war's over," knowing that it was inevitable that slavery would come to an end. Her husband and mother lived in ignorant, arrogant confidence that such a day would never come.

The housemaids at Miss Daisy's and Mrs. Willimina's lived under their roofs in more civilized conditions, not having to make the long trek morning and night to the outlying, freezing shacks. The drawback was, of course, that since they slept in the house in case they were needed during the night, they didn't live with their families, and were subject to their mistresses' demands twenty-four hours a day.

Em wondered what would be in store today, her heart a perpetual lump in her throat since discovering the truth about her family tree. The fear and helplessness on the plantation was contagious, but so was the hope and faith. Maybe this whole debacle wasn't an accident; maybe she had come to find her great-grandfather Noah Jackson . . . . And maybe she had come to save him.

But what would it mean when they went back home to 1945 and she and her friends knew the truth about her? She was colored. Did *that mean she had to use the colored drinking fountains and colored restrooms now? She was ashamed she'd never before given much thought to the segregation that was so prevalent in her world.*

Before she could fully grasp what her new knowledge about her identity entailed, everyone in the little shack was up and moving, eating stale bread and jam, saying prayers for the day, and heading off to the far corners of the Dunkelman farm. Em and Eliza walked briskly together to Miss Daisy's house, Em vigorously rubbing her aching hands together to warm them. An icy drizzle slid from the sky, coating every surface with a slick shimmer. Had Em been bundled up in her wool coat and mittens and her winter boots back home, she would have hoped for it to turn even colder so she could ice skate with her friends. But now the inclement weather just made for harder, more unbearable working conditions on the plantation.

Before Em could warm herself in the kitchen, Miss Daisy sent her to the Big House at Mrs. Willimina's request. Em considered running back to the Nolans' —if she could find it —but the weather gave her pause and she found herself considering staying long enough to find out how she could help the plantation slaves that she had learned were her family.

"You don' belong here," Gin said brusquely to Em, echoing Eliza's words as Em entered Mrs. Willimina's bustling kitchen.

Em kept her mouth shut, not sure how to respond.

"If you on the run, hate to see where you came from to end up here. Who you belong to?"

"Nobody," Em stammered. "I don't belong to anybody."

9

Down in Front

Maxine wasn't sure what she was doing. In a daze, she handed the attendant a ten dollar bill and was given a ticket in return. She didn't know what had emboldened her to try to—or even want to—go to what was most likely a white theater. And she knew she'd catch heck if her mama knew she'd just spent her lunch money on a movie ticket! She proceeded cautiously into the movie theater lobby, the cool air weighted with the hefty scent of buttered popcorn, the décor bold and garish. Purple, orange, and yellow patterns fought against each other, movie posters of smooth, perfect, shiny people who all looked the same stretched from floor to ceiling. Though everything looked shinier, it was the same as it always had been: beautiful, thin white people with smooth flowing hair gazed at her from every poster. Just like every magazine at the five and dime and every billboard. No one looked like her. She was constantly reminded that she was not, in the infamous Katie Hillman's words, *"normal."*

Maxine needed to think; normally a movie theater was the last place to do that, but now her sister was back in town and sharing her room, and everywhere else felt too much in the open.

She passed the snack counter and her mouth gaped when she saw the prices for popcorn and soda pop. Did she need glasses or was she reading that correctly? She shook her head in awe. She also noticed that nobody seemed to care that a colored girl was at this theater by herself. She wouldn't have dared to go to just any movie cinema in the 1950s; even the drive-in was risky. There had been a small theater a few blocks away where Negro folks went, but the new movies always went to the white theaters first. The small neighborhood theater, Maxine had noticed, had since been replaced by a cosmetic surgeon's business.

Maxine had discovered this cineplex, ostentatiously lit up in jewel tones and pulsating like a permanent concrete circus, when she had left the house and wandered aimlessly. No one would miss her; Melba was in their room listening to music (silently, with little cords running out of her ears) and her parents weren't back from work. After James had dropped her off at home, she found she couldn't sit still, her mind full of questions for and about her supposed friends.

She went into the romantic comedy for which she'd bought a ticket and, as was her habit, proceeded to the last row in back. When only a half dozen other people wandered in, Maxine had an idea. During the ear-splittingly loud previews, she got up from her seat and made her way to the aisle. Her heart pounding, she walked to the front, to the very first row. She glanced at the others in the theater, some fiddling with their phones, a couple talking to each other not even looking at the screen, and yet another couple stuffing popcorn into their mouths as if it were their last meal on earth. Nobody looked at her pointedly or stiffened ominously or yelled a warning or went to get an usher to tell her she couldn't sit in front.

Emboldened, she made her way to the middle seat of the first row and plopped into it with satisfaction, a wide smile on her face. She turned her head slowly, to see if anyone had noticed her yet. Still fiddling, talking and munching. She sat up a little taller.

The previews blared. Explosions on the screen shook the room. Maxine jumped, frightened, but laughing. Then a black couple jumped out of a helicopter, clinging to each other and kissing. Maxine's eyes widened in shock and wonderment and giggled more. Each new scene was louder and bolder than the next and she couldn't help but flinch. Soon she was absorbed in the spectacle of it all. She'd never gotten to sit in front before, but for goodness' sake, who would *want* to?

Suddenly she jumped up, an epiphany urging her to her feet.

"Down in front," someone muttered half-heartedly. She waved happily and went to another seat. In all, she sat in fourteen places throughout the course of the movie.

It wasn't that she *had* to sit in the back, in the middle, or in the front: it was that she had the choice. And maybe "Useless Generation" wasn't the best-written essay, but she wrote it because she *could*.

She was free to do what she wanted. And she was free to experience the consequences.

Maxine walked home with a skip in her step. Her thoughts were still disorganized, but now they didn't feel tethered to tragedy. She noticed her surroundings as if for the first time, taking note of the changes and seeing them as progressive and promising. The full-grown trees evidenced the endurance and tenacity of life. The big stores and huge parking lots just showed that people were more prosperous and life was full of conveniences like never before.

The warm late spring air felt luxurious against her skin. The sun was setting later and later, extending the days and shortening the nights. Dusk had settled around the town, but the excitement and anticipation of summer had people outside walking their dogs, working in their yards using the cooler hours of the last available light. Maxine breathed in deeply. She had no idea what was coming and didn't care. She thought of some scenes from the movie that Judy would have appreciated and felt magnanimous in forgiving her.

For only the second time in two years, Maxine thought of the white girl who had once been her friend, Christine Douglass. She had gotten into the habit of thinking she'd never had a white friend because of how things had ended with Christine. In the summers, Maxine had accompanied Melba and Conrad to "the ditch"—a pond at the back of an abandoned property at the edge of town. Many of the kids from the colored school that went to Maxine's church congregated there, swimming, making up games, and creating a benign ruckus for fun. Maxine didn't much appreciate getting wet, even when the heat of summer was too much to bear. She preferred to sit in the shade, read, watch the others, and ponder. Every once in a while, she'd call out observations and crack clever jokes that would put the older boys who were wiseacres to shame.

The first time Christine had wandered over, appearing from behind a dense hedgerow, Maxine had held her breath.

Everyone in the ditch and surrounding it had grown instantly still, wary of the white girl. "Can I play?" the girl had asked. Everyone had laughed at her, except Maxine. After realizing they really weren't going to let her play, the girl had wandered over to Maxine's spot under the overgrown wild pear tree.

"Why is your skin that color?" the girl had asked.

Maxine had felt her heart race and her temper flare. "Why's *yours*?" she'd snapped back.

The girl had earnestly looked at her own pale, bony arms and skinny legs. Shrugging, she had said, "I dunno. What's your name?"

"Are you gonna tattle that we're here?"

The girl had shaken her head no. "I'm glad to have the company, honestly."

Maxine had stared at her. *She must be kidding. Company?* No one even wanted her around.

"I'm Christine Marie Douglass. I live with my aunt and uncle on account of my parents are dead."

This last detail had endeared Christine to Maxine and she softened. "I'm Maxine."

"Why aren't you playing in the water, Maxine?"

"I'd rather exercise my brain than my lungs."

Christine had invited herself to sit down next to Maxine and they hadn't stopped talking until Melba and Conrad had pulled Maxine away at sunset to go home.

The next day, Christine had appeared again. They'd spent the rest of the summer talking about anything, everything, and nothing worth talking about, and sometimes playing in the water because Maxine knew that Christine wanted to and the others wouldn't let her without Maxine. Christine had asked to touch Maxine's hair, but not in the obnoxious way Katie Hillman at school had: Katie had asked after she had already been gingerly prodding Maxine's head like it was coated with a corrosive toxin. Then she had said, surprised, as if to no one—as if Maxine wasn't even there—"Why, her hair feels *normal.*" When Christine had asked to touch Maxine's hair, however, she'd said, "Do you want to touch mine, too?"

When summer had come around the next year, Maxine had looked forward to seeing Christine. Sure enough, a week in, Christine had showed up at the ditch again. She wasn't as bony, was more filled out, and also didn't seem as dingy; her hair had looked combed and her nails had been clean. Toward the end of summer, when she and Maxine had chatted, Christine had seemed to have one eye on the boys, and it had made Maxine sad to have to compete for her friend's attention.

The next summer, which was last year—well, 1954 anyway— Christine hadn't come to the ditch. The week after school started, Maxine—escorted by Conrad as she usually was whenever she was outside her own neighborhood—had spotted Christine outside the five and dime. She'd never seen Christine anywhere other than at the ditch and in her excitement, she'd rushed up to her, barely stopping herself from throwing her arms around Christine in an appreciative embrace. Christine's former dish-water hair was gleaming platinum blond and she wore bright red lipstick. Maxine hadn't noticed at first that she was with a handsome and icy-eyed white boy.

"Christine!" Maxine had exclaimed instead of hugging her long-lost friend.

Christine had looked uncomfortable. "Do I *know* you?"

Before Maxine could remind her, the cold-eyed guy had muttered, "I told you this was a dangerous neighborhood, Christy," followed by a terrible word aimed at Maxine.

Five minutes after *Christy* and her awful boyfriend had walked away, Maxine had still stood frozen on the sidewalk, stunned.

When Conrad had come to retrieve Maxine, he'd said, "Hey, wasn't that the white girl from the ditch?"

Maxine had responded, "It looked like her, but it was someone else."

Maxine had allowed herself a few tears before falling asleep that night, and then had vowed never to think of Christine again. Not even the good times, because they must have been a lie. Maxine didn't want to have to do the same thing with the Fifties Chix: erase them from her memory to wipe out the betrayal.

Once again, burying her memories of Christine, Maxine now arrived home from the movies and swung the back door open. Her cousin Conrad sat at the kitchen counter, hunkered over a large bowl of spaghetti with sauce, scarfing it down. Maxine smiled a hello, simultaneously wondering where Conrad put all the food he ate. He gave her a funny look. Just as it was registering that he was shooting her a warning sign, Maxine's parents stormed in the room, closely followed by her sister.

"Girl! Where you been?" bellowed her mom. As she had done during the movie trailers, Maxine started.

"I—I—was at the movies," stammered Maxine.

"The *movies*??" Her mom over-pronounced the word.

"Well, yeah, no one was home from work yet and I—"

Conrad and her father gestured that it would be best if Maxine stopped talking.

"Do you want to tell us about this?" Her mother snapped *The Invisible Truth* in Maxine's face.

She was tempted to say, *What about it?* but stopped herself. She knew it wasn't her turn to talk, even if Mama had just asked her a question.

"We get a call from the principal on voicemail saying you threatened some poor girl, been bullying everyone—"

Now Maxine spoke up, her indignation too difficult to restrain. "Mama! I never threatened or bullied anybody!"

"The principal says you met with a teacher and another student and you called the girl names." Gloria put her hands on her hips and challenged Maxine to disagree.

"I might have called her an airhead—"

As her dad tried to stifle a smile, her mom simultaneously exclaimed, "Maxine Estelle!" while swatting her husband with the underground rag.

"Who was it?" Conrad piped up.

"Boy, you best keep your mouth shut," Gloria warned.

"Diane," Maxine answered him.

"Diane *Dunkelman?*" Conrad laughed something between an incredulous guffaw and a pleased whoop, his eyes big. *Nobody* messed with Diane Dunkelman, if they knew what was good for them. Whatever the circumstances were between his cousin and Diane, he was sure Diane deserved it. And he was sure that whatever Diane did to retaliate, Maxine would not deserve.

"I told you," Melba said knowingly to Maxine behind her parents.

"You knew about this?" Gloria's attention turned to her other daughter. "We'll be talking to you *later.*" Melba wisely clammed up. No matter how old she was, when she was under her mama's roof, she would comply with her wishes.

"Do you want to hear my side of the story?" Maxine urged, with the slightest tone of impatience.

"Your side?" Gloria roared. "Girl, there aren't sides. There's only one side, the *truth*."

Maxine explained, "I wrote an essay—*anonymously*—and that girl, that bad-news Diane Dunkelman, doesn't like me or my friends and she's trying to find a way to get one or all of us into trouble."

"And how did it come down to name-calling? We didn't teach you to stoop to that level!"

"Diane Dunkelman said the essay was racist against whites so Mrs. Fairview called Diane and me in after class to talk. Diane— she was the one making threats to Mrs. Fairview, who didn't do anything wrong. You know Mrs. F, Conrad, she's the most!" Maxine called for back up.

"The most . . . what?" Conrad said.

"Just . . . the *most*. Never mind. The point is, I was sticking up for Mrs. Fairview."

"You don't need to be sticking up for your teachers. They should be sticking up for you," her mother objected.

"You don't understand!" Maxine heard herself on the verge of howling.

"We're trying to understand, Maxine. But you've been acting different lately. Dressing strange, sneaking around a lot, writing this essay . . . ."

"Have you *read* the essay?" Maxine asked.

"Of course we have. But we want to know why would you want to get people all stirred up."

"Because it matters," Maxine stated fervently.

"Just because we have a black president—" Gloria started, but was interrupted by her daughter.

"It has nothing to do with who's president or who's not. I wrote it because I can. Because the Constitution of the United States of America says I can! I'm an American with rights."

With that, Maxine stalked out of the kitchen and through the house to her room. She slammed the door, instantly regretting possibly getting her mother more vexed. She prayed Melba wouldn't come in with an "I told you so" speech because she really wasn't up for it.

She collapsed on her bed and reached for her great-grandmother's quill on the desk next to her. She contemplated it, wondering once again what it had been like for Gin Harrison, a slave one day and free the next. Yet even when she was technically free, she must have been haunted by the trappings of slavery the rest of her life.

A knock came at the door and Maxine's heart swelled with fear. Her mother was certainly not done with Maxine yet. Without an acknowledgment or invitation, Mama opened the door and came in.

She came and sat on the end of Maxine's bed, watching her hold the quill.

"Believe it or not, things used to be even more difficult," her mom said. She was speaking more gently than Maxine had anticipated.

"I *know*," Maxine said in agreement. Still . . . things weren't so easy now, either.

"Can you imagine what she went through?" her mom asked, referring to Gin, the original owner of the quill.

"No," Maxine said. "Mama, I wasn't trying to be disrespectful writing that essay or in the way that I spoke to anyone . . . ."

"I know you weren't, Max. You are something special, girl; I don't know if the world's ready for you yet, is all. But . . . even if they're not, you promise me you won't hold back?"

Tears sprung to Maxine's eyes. How she longed to tell her mom about what she was going through . . . all of it. But there was a catch in her throat and even if she could find the words, they just weren't coming out.

"Don't you sit down or stand up or shut up or speak out unless God Himself tells you, you hear me, Max?"

Maxine nodded and her mama wrapped her in a hug so big, she felt it all the way back in 1955.

10

Divided and Conquered

"So . . . how do you feel about all this 'Useless Generation' hype?"

Conrad caught Bev off guard. They rarely talked about anything other than baseball, especially at baseball practice. He'd jogged up next to her as they were running laps. In two days, they had a district championship game they were focusing on winning.

"What do you mean, how do I *feel* about it?"

"You know, you for it or against it?"

"Maxine is my friend, so whatever you're asking, I stand by her." Bev didn't like to socialize while she was running; she had just gotten into a rhythm where she could start to think about pushing herself harder.

"Just so you know, Dunk is out to get her."

"Diane Dunkelman?" Bev almost tripped. Why did Conrad look like he wasn't exerting himself at all? He might as well be lounging on the sofa with a book, he looked so relaxed. Fine; Bev could keep this up all day. She picked up the pace.

"Yeah, I guess she and Mrs. F and Maxine all had a meeting yesterday after school. It didn't go so well. Dunkelman egged her on—you know how she does—and long story short, the principal called home last night saying Maxine called her a name, threatened her, stuff like that. My aunt and uncle are pretty ticked."

Bev almost came to a dead stop. That's what Maxine had been talking about yesterday afternoon when they were all at Judy's. No wonder Maxine had left in a huff; Bev should have gone after her. And today in current events, Maxine had kept quietly to herself. Bev felt stupid for having to learn this from Conrad, but she was also grateful he was looking to her to help. Her mind raced with not very nice ideas on how to silence Diane Dunkelman once and for all.

"So . . . you'll help my cousin?" Conrad had a pleading look and he suddenly appeared much younger. Bev got a glimpse of what an adorable little boy he must have been.

"Of course!" She was almost indignant, embarrassed that she hadn't been in orbit sooner.

"Just checking, because you know, your brother . . ." Conrad gestured up ahead, to the leader of the pack, seven runners between them. There was Bob, out front, but struggling like Bev. Neither one of them especially liked running.

"What about him?"

"He's kinda torqued about that essay."

"What?" Now Bev did stumble. Conrad instinctively reached out to steady her without breaking his stride.

"Let's bring it in," Coach called from the infield. The runners veered off, leaving Bev and Conrad, who both slowed.

Bev didn't know what to say, but she wanted to assure Conrad that she would never abandon Maxine. Or him.

"My brother . . ." she started.

" . . . can be kind of a jerkwad?" Conrad finished.

"I wasn't going to say *that*," Bev said, her defenses rising. She could call her brother a fream, but she wasn't going to let anyone else.

"So you don't have a problem with him being a bigot?"

"Marshall, Jenkins! Let's go!" Coach hollered.

Conrad peeled off with the rest of the team toward the coach.

"Bigot? Are you out of your mind? Bob is not a *bigot!*"

"You might want to tell him that," Conrad called over his shoulder.

"Yeah? Well, you Marshalls might want to cool it with the name-calling!" Bev yelled, louder than she meant to. The team turned to stare at her. Except for Conrad, who didn't look back at all.

Have I somehow just indirectly defended Diane Dunkelman with that statement? Ohhh, that Conrad, Bev thought. She could just scream!

"There you are. Why do I get the feeling you're avoiding me?" James kept it light, laughing as he said it, but he sounded a little worried and behind his freckles, his skin looked a little more flushed than normal.

Mary shoved her books in her locker and pulled out others she'd need for homework that night. She'd been doing lots of homework since she had more time now that she'd given back the mechanical baby. And since she wanted to block out constant thoughts of James O'Grady.

"I'm not avoiding you," she lied coolly. Then she felt awful. Why did she have to be ill-mannered? Couldn't she find some graceful way to make him just go away . . . or better yet, couldn't she just evaporate into thin air?

James stiffened and his chin jutted out slightly. The moment had come. He knew exactly what this was about: that ridiculous poem. Maybe that stupid rag should be renamed from *The Invisible Truth* to *The Divisible Truth*. He wanted to explain it to her; but it was after all, a poem. It should speak for itself.

He cleared his throat and said weakly, "Anything you want to talk about?"

Mary shook her head, as if getting hair out of her eyes, but it was all gathered up in her typically well-groomed ponytail. "No, thank you. I think I'll just go . . . *write a poem about it.* Excuse me." She slammed her locker door and flounced away.

He called after her, "Mary!" and was surprised when she stopped. But the words that came out of his mouth were not what he'd planned: "Be good to Maxine; she needs you right now."

When Mary turned back to face him, he'd already started walking away. That boy was infuriating!

❖　　❖　　❖

"I'm sorry, but I just don't see it," Gary said. He was watching his brother and sister at baseball practice; really it was an excuse to be outdoors instead of locked up inside, pounding away on his laptop writing his final about the Balkans for AP History. It was a bonus that he'd run into Ann, who'd accompanied her friend, Judy.

Judy squinted up at Gary and then glanced out at the field. She should have just let go of this whole "Useless Generation" thing, but she'd overheard Bob complaining about it to a couple of the guys at lunch. Unfortunately, they'd been gathered around Diane Dunkelman at the time. Everyone at school was talking about it. When Gary had joined them in the bleachers, Judy had asked his opinion about the essay that everyone now knew her friend had written.

"That's because there's nothing *to* see," Ann said in response to Gary. She was frustrated that Judy's loyalties were divided, and if not divided, so easily rattled. How could she possibly question Maxine after all that the five of them had been through together? Judy was like a magnet for drama. But this was real life . . . or something close to it.

"Why do you think everyone's freaking out about it?" Gary asked as an excuse to keep the conversation with Ann going. He had a million other things he wanted to ask her, but this would do for now.

Ann took off her hat, fanning herself with it, the curled tufts of brown hair around her face flapping up and down with the makeshift breeze. "Because people care more about controversy than they do about other people."

Gary smiled. He'd already written at least two songs inspired by Ann and he could see more lyrics forming around that comment.

To keep her talking, he said, "And what is the controversy here?"

Ann looked annoyed, as if she thought Gary was challenging her. "Obviously that anyone who doesn't fit into some picture perfect Hollywood image—"

"Hey!" Judy protested.

"—is somehow a threat and should just sit down and shut up so as not to rock the boat. I mean, listen to how beautiful this line is that she wrote: *We should learn that peace is not a silencing of the disaffected minority, but a willingness within each of us to listen and care even when we don't agree or understand.* How could that be controversial?"

Judy was visibly affected. Her jaw clenched and she blinked back tears. She felt Ann's words had been carefully chosen just for her. She stood up, brushing the back of her skirt brusquely. "I think I'll start walking home now."

Ann regretted her tone and her words. She knew there was a better way to deal with Judy. "Wait," she said.

But Judy was already making her way down the bleachers, her pale yellow pigtails bright in the sun.

Ann turned on Gary. "Why'd you do that?" she questioned, her eyebrows knit together.

He hadn't seen this side of her. "I didn't do anything," he said.

"Yes, you did. You were needling me and trying to get me to say something mean. I walked right into your trap. You're just like everyone else, you care about controversy more than people!" She pulled her hat onto her head a little too hard and there was a ripping sound. She flung it off, inspecting a tear, and said, "Now look what you've done!"

She strode off angrily, leaving Gary alone and befuddled.

11

"My Heart Shall not Fear . . . "

May and Row mucked out the stalls for the mules Lachlan raised and sold to the Union army. May's back ached and her hands were raw, and they were still hours from a lunch break (or "dinner", as Fiona called it). Normally, Lachlan's hired hands would be doing this work, Fiona explained, but they were busy constructing another outbuilding before the onslaught of winter. Besides, hired help was hard to come by with so many boys and men either off at war or indisposed due to injuries from the war. It made May think of the job her mother had held in a factory, along with millions of other women, when the men went off to World War II. Eighty percent of the women had lost their jobs as soon as the war ended. People forgot that wars weren't fought just by men.

Lachlan had a big black and brown dog who looked exactly like Finigan, whom he in fact even called Finigan. Row explained this strange coincidence with the fact that Finigan was a good Irish name and maybe it had been a family pet name passed along over the generations. Not surprisingly, the new Fin (or was it the old one?) had taken an instant liking to Row. But Row was wise enough not to ask to bring Finigan inside. He slept in the barn with the other animals. Finigan followed closely on Row's heels whenever Row was outside.

"I'm going to go get Em and bring her back here," May announced to Row.

Row wiped her forehead, moving her hair, once smooth and glamorous but now stringy and frayed-looking, out of her eyes. She understood now why Fiona's hair was always braided and tucked into a bonnet. "Do you have a plan for doing that?"

May paused to lean on the heavy pitchfork, taking shallow breaths between her teeth to keep the sharp ammonia smell out of her nose. "I don't know; just go get her. And wind the watch and go home."

"If it were as simple as winding the watch, wouldn't we already be home? And do you know where the Jackson plantation is?" Row objected.

Row went back to shoveling soiled hay into the wheelbarrow. She'd learned the hard way yesterday to not fill it too full. On her way to the manure pile, she'd dumped the teetering wheelbarrow and had to take two subsequent trips to properly dispose of it. Today, with the sleet coming down, she didn't want to take any longer than necessary. She sighed, "I know what you meant and I'm sorry for barking at you. I'm just scared, May."

May took a quiet moment after Row's admission. Row never spoke of her feelings, especially something so dark and intimate as fear. Should she pretend she hadn't heard it? Should she reassure Row that there was nothing to be afraid of? May's honesty ultimately betrayed her and she admitted, "So am I, and I know Emily is, too."

"That's not what I mean. I mean, yes, I'm scared of what's going on here and how we got here; but I'm also scared to go back. I don't have anyone to go back to; Mom's gone and I miss the boys something awful. Dad's got Gladys now and even her wretched daughter, Grace. I just feel . . . lost."

For all the days and nights they'd spent together, all the summer days on the porch, all the evenings by the fire, the long walks to the soda fountain, May had never heard Row speak about such raw feelings like this. May had learned to not ask questions or make demands from Row, and here Row was, volunteering the information. Now May knew she needed not only to extricate Emily, she also needed to rescue Rowena in some sense.

The previous night, May had searched for a way to wind the watch, and, finding none, clung to it and wished and prayed with all her might that it would take them back to good old 1945. When she had again woken up to that blasted rooster, she wondered if she hadn't wished hard enough, held the watch in the right way, or prayed with enough fervency. With a pain in her heart, she thought of the words she'd heard her dad speak on many occasions: God always answers our prayers, Marionberry. It's just that sometimes the answer is no.

"I declare, what is that dreadful squeaking sound?" Mrs. Shelby Jackson was in a foul mood. She slammed her embroidery down, sending strands of silky, brightly colored floss rippling out like tiny banners in a breeze.

Emily straightened up. "Ma'am?" she asked politely through a tightened jaw.

A little after lunch it had started to snow and Emily was grateful to be inside, or that's what she kept telling herself. Every time she returned to Gin in the kitchen to help prepare supper for the Jacksons—and the "visiting" Dunkelmans—Mrs. Jackson would have a conniption about one thing or another. Her dearly departed mother's art glass lamp was too full of oil; her dearly departed mother's art glass lamp was too low on oil; she spotted dust on her dearly departed mother's painted portrait over the fireplace; the fire in the fireplace was crackling too much and it should be roaring instead. She'd even demanded the curtains be closed because she didn't want cold air seeping in, then was upset that she couldn't watch the snow fall with the curtains drawn closed.

On one such visit, Mrs. Jackson complained of having the "vapors" and Emily learned firsthand that there was nothing quaint or vaguely romantic about a lady with the vapors. Mrs. Jackson had gas. And of course she complained about the smell in the room, naturally wanting fresh air—but without any windows being opened.

A lady from Mrs. Jackson's big church in the city sat with her, working very hard on an embroidery piece featuring a Bible quote: "The Lord is my light and my salvation; whom shall I fear? The Lord is the stronghold of my life; of whom shall I be afraid? Though an army encamp against me, my heart shall not fear; though war rise up against me, yet I will be confident. Psalm 27: 1, 3" and an image of the Confederate flag. Her hoop skirt was so large, it stood at attention, perpendicular to the floor when she sat. White-haired Mrs. Bondurant—Emily had had to figure out her name on her own because of course they weren't introduced—had to fight the skirt and its ostentatious ruffles with every laborious stitch on her embroidery. She was only distracted from her stitching work long enough to glare at Emily with distaste, then make a clucking sound. Em didn't know if the woman was mute, or merely rude.

And now Mrs. Jackson was demanding about the squeaking sound as Em was opening the curtains for the third time.

"Walk over here, girl," Mrs. Jackson ordered.

Em tiptoed over.

"Why, it is your shoes! Those silly shoes! Take them off at once. You are giving me a headache with that awful racket." She gestured impatiently.

Em leaned over, reluctant to remove her shoes. She had pried off the bows yesterday, and the burgundy leather already looked years older with thin cracks caked with clay. Her peep toe wedgies were nothing like the boots everyone else wore, or the makeshift sandals she saw some of the slaves around the plantation wear. Every time she looked at her feet in these shoes, she felt like a dancer. If she couldn't wear her ballet point shoes, she could don these. She had been loathe to part with them, even if they must have looked very silly to everyone else, especially, as it turned out, Mrs. Jackson.

She stepped out of her shoes and picked them up.

"Bring them here," directed Mrs. Jackson.

Em's now bare feet were rooted to the pine-planked floor.

"I said, bring them," hissed Mrs. Jackson. Mrs. Bondurant looked incredulous, clearly judging Mrs. Jackson for not having more a compliant housemaid.

"I—but—these are my shoes," Em stuttered.

Mrs. Bondurant dropped her embroidery project in utter shock at Em's backtalk.

Now Mrs. Jackson was raging and flew from her seat, her large skirt springing and swaying around her absurdly. Her face was red and puffy in an instant, her narrow blue eyes as sharp and shiny as broken glass. She hurled herself at Em, who unexpectedly let out a whimper.

"You listen and obey when I talk to you!" screeched Mrs. Jackson.

"Why, what is all the fuss about?" came a smooth deep voice from the double doors.

Mrs. Jackson whirled around to see her son-in-law, Crawford, with her daughter, Daisy, on his arm. He was unfazed while she looked horrified. She'd always been a sensitive child. Too sensitive, Willimina repeatedly said.

"This girl," Mrs. Jackson spat, "is trying to kill me!"

Em gasped. She couldn't look anywhere else in the well-appointed, expensively decorated room than at Daisy, who seemed the only rational human being in the world at that moment. Which was saying a lot.

"Oh, Mama," Daisy said, going into placate mode.

"Mrs. Willimina, please do not hurt yourself. Why, you let me take care of this. Do not think another thing about it. Just sit down before this creature causes you any more injury." In a few rapid strides, like a snake striking its prey before you can even see it move, Crawford crossed the room, releasing Mrs. Jackson's grip on Em and replacing it with his own harsh grasp.

As he wrestled Em toward the door, Gin appeared from the kitchen to see what the commotion was. Her eyes looked big and frightened, which scared Em even more. She felt as though the blood had drained from her body and she had lost control of her limbs. Crawford dragged her and she stumbled through the hall, the front door and down the porch steps outside and into the snow. Her threw her down and she fell on her backside; as she stared at him through her knees, she realized that her shoes were still in the parlor and her only thought was not of physical safety, but of getting her shoes back.

"Let us see if we cannot work this out," Crawford drawled. He smoothed his hair, then twisted his big yellow mustache. It was thin and long, a source of misplaced pride.

He had a gleam in his eye then that made Em promptly forget about her shoes.

Gin burst out the front door and stopped short.

"No!" cried Em before she could stop herself. She wanted Gin to go back inside and stay out of it for her Gin's own safety.

"I see how it is," said Crawford, his eyes darting between Emily and Gin, a dim recognition in his soulless eyes. "See, when you do not do what Mrs. Willimina say, she gonna git it." He had pitted his slaves against each other before to his great success in coercion and control.

With the back of his hand, he slapped Gin across the face hard and Em leapt to her feet. Crawford then struck Em and pushed them both to the ground. He straightened his coat and rubbed a finger across his teeth, as if he'd just bitten into something messy. "Miss Virginia, when can we 'spect supper?" He said it sweetly, as if the cook wasn't lying in the wintry mud he'd just shoved her into.

"Right quick, sir," Gin answered, playing along as though she were not the cook he'd just heaved onto the ground.

"We clear now?" he asked Em with a smile.

She couldn't speak, so she just nodded twice. By the second nod, he had turned to go back into the house and something began to grow in her that couldn't be stopped. A red hot inferno, starting deep within and raging like an uncontrollable wildfire right out to the tips of her fingers and icy toes. It wasn't anger, no, that was too one-dimensional; it was something much more significant. She had been overwhelmed and fearful—selfish, even—in her willingness to go along with this lifestyle in order to be with her newfound family; but the selfishness of that was consumed in the blazing within her. No, it wasn't hate in that heated moment barefoot in the snow when she dedicated herself to freeing her family and her future.

It was love.

The words stitched with such irreverence on Mrs. Bondurant's linen swatch embroidered themselves tidily onto Em's heart and became a battle call: *Though an army encamp against me, my heart shall not fear; though war rise up against me, yet I will be confident.*

She knew what she had to do.

12

That's How Rumors Get Started

That night, Judy got on her Facebook account hoping to "run into" Bob. She was feeling lonely and out of sorts. She was embarrassed that she hadn't immediately come right out and stuck up for Maxine; but all those kids at school—including Bob —couldn't be wrong, could they? She'd read Maxine's essay again and didn't understand what was wrong with it. But she didn't totally understand it, either. If she took Maxine's side, her chances with Bob could be ruined. She wondered distantly what Bev thought, since Bev was Bob's sister. Bev wasn't like Judy; Bev avoided conflict, and so it was hard for Judy to tell what Bev honestly felt. Then there was Diane Dunkelman. Judy couldn't possibly agree with anything that Diane Dunkelman believed!

As soon as Diane appeared in Judy's line of reasoning, her name appeared on the screen. *Diane Shelby Dunkelman* requesting Judy's friendship! Judy's heart skipped a beat. Diane was intimidating and had her unappealing moments, but she was the most popular girl in school, and that counted for something. None of Judy's friends liked Diane. She wondered what they would think if they knew she was friends with her on Facebook. She felt a prickle of something in the pit of her stomach. Maybe it was rebelliousness. She didn't have to run everything by her friends. They certainly didn't run everything by her! She hadn't known about Maxine's essay until after the fact, and even then, they had all treated her with exasperation, even usually kind and soft-spoken Ann. Instead of treating Judy like she was a fool, they could have just explained the controversy to her!

In a moment of defiance, Judy sucked in her breathe and hit "confirm." Diane's name was instantly added to Judy's very short list of friends. She'd only cared about being friends with Bob. She sat for a brief moment, wondering if she'd just made a mistake, when Bob's name popped up on screen.

"What r u doing?" he asked.

She thought for a minute about what he'd like to hear. She didn't want to bring up the topic of Maxine. She thought of the thing that had got them to talking in the first place.

"Thinking about my dad," she wrote back.

"Me too!" he agreed. "Thinking about the military that is."

Judy grinned; she'd written the right thing.

Just then her computer dinged and another conversation screen popped up.

"Hey girl." It was Diane Dunkelman!

Judy jumped out of her chair and backed away from the computer screen. She knew, or she thought she knew, that no one could see her and she hoped she was right that no one—Diane—could see who else she was talking to: Bob. Judy stared at the screen, wringing her hands nervously. She never should have accepted Diane's friend invitation.

"What do I do?" she asked Dragnet. She was in the habit of asking her cats for advice, even though they had yet to offer anything helpful. Dragnet didn't even lift his head from his nap. For a brief moment, she even thought of asking her mom, but she was in her room falling asleep with the TV on. She'd worked late, then had a late dinner date with her boss, stayed on the computer working some more, and asked Judy about her day. Judy had answered with her standard "fine," and Bitsy had smiled absently and gone to her room. Gone were the days where Bitsy and Judy had curled up on the sofa to eat TV dinners and watch *I Love Lucy*. Judy tried not to think about it. It made her too sad.

Now she took two deep breaths and settled back in front of the computer. Shaking her hands out, then settling her fingers onto the "ASDF-G/H-JKL;" position, she carefully typed back, "Hi, Diane."

"what r u doing right noww gf"

Judy puzzled over the spelling and lack of punctuation in Diane's message—"gf," was that even supposed to be a word? Judy sure wasn't going to divulge that she had another conversation going with Bob.

"Typing a message to you," she wrote back to Diane.

Bob's conversation box blinked.

"whats the deal with the marshalls. U no maxine whats her deal. bev wont talk about it." Judy shook her head a few times quickly, hoping to clear the cobwebs and understand just what it was Bob was typing. *Did no one use punctuation or grammar in the future?* she wondered. This kind of thing would drive Mary bananas!

"hahaha rofl," Diane now responded in the other box. Now she was just typing nonsense, Judy figured.

"What are you doing?" Judy typed back to Diane's box. She was still trying to work out what to say to Bob.

"avoiding hw as per usuallll," Diane's box responded.

How was this supposed to be enjoyable? Judy puzzled. It hurt her brain. What in the world was hw? As soon as she thought it, it came: *homework*. It had to be.

"I know, me too!" she typed, triumphant.

"bev not talking to YOU?," came the quick response from Bob.

Judy gasped. *Oh no!* She had sent the message to Bob instead of Diane.

She quickly typed, "No, Bev is fine."

"ur with beverly??" Now there was punctuation . . . but Judy had done it again. She had once more typed her response into the wrong box; the question marks came from Diane's message. What Judy had meant for Bob now had gone to Diane. And Diane must have thought Judy was sitting there with Bev!

"Noooo!" Judy wailed, throwing her arms onto the desk and her head on top of her arms.

"No, I thought you meant something else. I'm sorry. I'm still new to Facebook. You must think I am such a L7!" Judy typed very carefully into her response area to Diane.

"whats L7."

"Ha!" Judy laughed. *Now you know how I feel*, she thought, but typed, "A square."

"whatevs," came Diane's response, and then she evidently logged off.

Judy went back to focusing on her conversation with Bob. Before she could type her brilliant response, he too had logged off.

"I hate Facebook," Judy said and logged herself out. She felt queasy and nervous. If she had wondered about friending Diane Dunkelman earlier, she had no doubts now: she never should have clicked on that "confirm" option.

"What's happening?" Judy asked the first person she saw, Katie Hillman. As soon as she had approached the school the next morning, she'd spotted police officers swarming every entrance.

"Stupid threat called in," Katie sighed. She was chomping gum like it was what kept her heart beating. She rolled her eyes and twirled her hair, a sleek ponytail held in place by a chiffon scarf. She wore pedal pushers and a crisp blouse.

"What does that mean?" Judy heard her voice squeak.

"I dunno . . . somebody saw some lame post on Facebook or whatever. Oh, super *cute*!" Katie pointed distractedly at the fake pearl necklace Judy had around her neck.

"Thanks," Judy said, passing Katie and pushing through the crowd. A sickening feeling was mushrooming in her stomach. Near the bottom of the wide concrete steps that led to the main entrance, Judy spotted Bev. Relieved, she made her way to her friend.

"Beverly! What's going on?"

Bev, standing on a step up from Judy, suddenly seemed to tower over Judy. "Why did you tell Bob we aren't on speaking terms?" Her normally mellow hazel eyes were blazing.

Judy was taken aback. She knew what Bev was referring to, of course, her blunder with Bob on Facebook last night, but she didn't know why Bev was so miffed. "I didn't—I didn't mean to . . . ."

"If you like drama, you should be very happy now. Look how out of control this has gotten!"

Judy had only ever seen Bev aggressive on the field. When Bev was fired up like this, she was even more intimidating than . . . than Diane Dunkelman. Judy didn't know if she should snap back at Bev or burst out in tears.

Judy looked around her. "My stars! You don't think this is all about Maxine—"

"Of course it is! Now if you'll excuse me, I'm going to go try to find my *friend*, Maxine."

Bev made her way up the stairs and Judy watched as a police officer questioned her and looked through Bev's knapsack and paper lunch bag. Bev had never looked so vexed. Once past the officer, Bev stormed through the double doors and was swallowed up into the brick building.

Judy's throat was dry and she felt dizzy. Even as the crowd of kids buzzing loudly with curiosity jostled her to and fro, she had the sense that she was utterly alone.

❖　　❖　　❖

"Wear this," Ann said. It was a strange thing to do and she wasn't entirely sure where the idea had come from, but she removed her necklace with the Star of David and offered it to her friend.

Maxine's eyes glistened. She had been unmoved until this tender gesture. Instead of taking Ann's necklace, however, her hands went behind her own neck and she unclasped her own gold necklace with the cross. She held it out to Ann.

They traded necklaces and put each other's on, smiling.

"Looks good on you," Maxine said.

"You, too." Ann nodded her approval. She gave Maxine a quick hug. "This will all get straightened out, I promise."

"Maxine?" Principal Jones opened the door to his office and gestured for Maxine. Ann was grateful she had seen Maxine heading into the school office this morning after all the chaos she'd experienced just getting through the main entrance into school. There were police who refused to let her wear her hat and looked through her bag, after she'd waited in line for twenty minutes. It was like a crime scene or a police state.

Ann had wanted to sit with Maxine after Maxine had explained she'd been called to the principal's office. Ann had said she wanted to go in to see the principal with her, but the school secretary had refused, saying that the principal would call Maxine in alone.

Now, Maxine gave Ann's hand a quick squeeze and bravely walked into Principal Jones's office, her shoulders squared and her head held high. How Ann was filled with pride watching her friend! She leaned as close to the door as she could to listen. For several minutes, she heard the murmur of Mr. Jones's voice, but even when it paused, she could not hear Maxine's. With every silent beat, Ann leaned even closer, almost off her chair entirely, until the door swung open and she nearly collapsed onto the floor.

"Have you gotten a hold of either of the Marshalls yet?" the principal bellowed to the secretaries. They stared at him blankly. Mr. Jones turned his attention to Ann. "Will you come sit with her and help her answer some questions until one of her parents gets here?" he asked.

Ann's voice failed her, so she nodded her head eagerly and jumped up.

The principal escorted her into his office and gestured at the chair next to Maxine's.

Ann sat, her hands clasped in her lap primly. She would have been scared, except that she was here for her friend and this made her feel brave.

"Name?" Principal Jones grunted.

"Oh. Me? Ann. Well, Anna. Branislav."

He tapped something onto the keyboard on his desk and looked over the top of his glasses at her.

"Anna," Principal Jones started. Out of the corner of her eye, Ann sensed Maxine shake her head every so slightly as if to say no. Ann didn't know if she was imagining it until the principal continued. "Your friend Maxine is in a lot of trouble, but she is being smart with me. I've asked her several questions and she won't answer. She said she doesn't know what Facebook is. I'm hoping you, as her friend, can help her understand that this is not a game. Her locker's been searched, but the second her parents get here . . . . Ann, do you know about Maxine's threat on Facebook?"

"I'm not sure . . . I don't know what that is." Ann felt her cheeks go hot, scared for her friend and embarrassed she couldn't help.

"Another one," the principal sighed. He took off his glasses and massaged the bridge of his nose. The gray wispy hairs that circled the lower half of his bald head like a fuzzy crown danced in an invisible breeze. "Your flippancy tells me you both wouldn't mind being suspended or expelled?"

Ann's heart dropped and her eyes strayed toward Maxine. Still Maxine said nothing, so neither did Ann.

The principal swiveled his computer screen around to show Ann and Maxine. "Can you just nod yes or no if this is your account, Maxine?"

Ann didn't know what she was looking at, but there was a picture of a regal Negro woman she didn't know on the upper left hand corner of the screen and several lines of text broken up by white space. On the top line of text, Ann caught the words "gun to school." Her mouth gaped open and her eyes widened. Was Maxine being accused of threatening to bring a gun to school? Anybody vaguely familiar with Maxine would immediately see how ludicrous that was.

Ann started to protest, but Maxine spoke first. "'*It is dangerous to be right in matters on which the established authorities are wrong.*'"

"I don't know what that means," the principal said blandly.

"It's Voltaire," Maxine said by way of explanation.

Despite the panic rising within her, Ann had to try to keep from smiling.

"Your parents had better be more willing to explain what is going on here when they arrive. We don't take these threats lightly; when the police are called in, the community wants someone to be held accountable."

Ann's heart raced. She knew Maxine was innocent of whatever the school was accusing her of, but she was afraid of what would happen if Maxine didn't speak up soon. As she tried to gather her thoughts and defend her friend, Principal Jones dismissed her.

"But—" Ann said.

Maxine grabbed her hand and squeezed it again, her lips pressed together in a secret smile. She wanted Ann to go. Ann did as her friend desired, but walking away and thinking of Maxine throughout the day was torture.

There was a general feeling of discontent and chaos at school. Rumors were flying like annoying mosquitos buzzing by your ears no matter how much you try to wave them away. Over and over again, Ann heard Maxine's name mentioned. She felt utterly powerless; when she tried to speak up to defend Maxine, no one was interested in what she had to say because she wasn't perpetuating the spectacle. When fifth period arrived and Maxine never showed, it took every shred of dignity and restraint Ann had to not weep with worry right there in front of everyone.

She touched the cross at the base of her throat. She and Maxine had the same God; and they needed Him to intervene now more than ever.

13

Make New Friends, Keep the Old

At lunch, Judy wasn't sure she would be welcome to sit with her friends, Ann and Beverly. She stood with her tray of hot, limp pizza and cut-up, under-ripe apple slices and considered ditching her lunch and sitting in the library until fifth period. Except that she'd still have to face her friends in Mrs. F's current events class.

"Judy!"

She glanced up hopefully, her heart skipping a beat. But it wasn't Ann or Bev who had called her. Diane Dunkelman flagged her down. She was sitting with her friend Carla DiFrancisco at a table full of boys, including Bob Jenkins. Judy hesitated, but Diane waved again. And then Bob looked up and nodded hello to her. Her feet moved without her permission toward their table.

A few guys shoved over to give her some space and she squeezed in with her tray. Diane laughed a innocent-sounding giggle. "Is that how you keep your *girly* figure? I always wondered," and pointed at Judy's pizza. Judy blushed. Diane's emphasis on the word girly seemed to imply the opposite of feminine and appealing.

"Don't listen to her, she's just jealous," Carla said, not bothering to look up, her nose buried in her cell phone. Judy sucked her breath in, waiting for Diane's wrath, but the two girls only laughed and Diane playfully told Carla to shut up. They both fiddled with their phones, sending secret messages. Judy noticed they didn't have lunch trays; just one diet soda pop each. The guys, on the other hand, had heaps of food: pizza, sandwiches, and breaded chicken strips, enough to feed an army. They too, were texting on their phones while leaning back precariously on only one or two legs of their chairs.

"Hi, Bob," Judy ventured.

"Hey," he said, grabbing a banana off another kid's tray as his chair clattered against the table. Judy noticed a sudden and distinct chill from Diane's direction.

"So, Judy," Diane said, speaking too loudly. "Tell us about this little *fashiontrend* you've started." She waved her hand dismissively at Judy's clothes and then texted something. Judy realized she had just texted Carla because Carla's phone buzzed and Carla giggled under her breath.

Judy blushed again and picked up an apple slice for something to do, then put it back down. "Oh, it's not . . . I didn't really . . . ."

"Are you gonna eat that?" one of the baseball players asked Judy, pointing to her pizza.

Judy shook her head no, afraid to speak up for fear her voice would crack. She should be thrilled to be sitting with the popular kids, especially with Bob Jenkins, but she was scared to death. In fact, she was praying she didn't throw up on the spot. But things only got worse.

Diane lowered her voice and leaned across the table conspiratorially toward Judy. The others at the table got quiet and paused playing with their phones long enough to hear what Diane was going to say (and then pass it on electronically, presumably). "So, what is the *deal* with Maxine Marshall?"

Judy's face got hot for what felt like the hundredth time since Diane had waved her over and she shrugged. The kids at the table all looked over at Conrad Marshall—the closest thing they could find to Maxine, since Maxine had a different lunch period. Conrad sat with Duncan Marsalis, the catcher on the baseball team; James O'Grady; and a couple of other kids. Conrad made a point of looking away when the whole table where Judy sat stared at him, but he didn't look happy.

Judy needn't have worried because the focus wasn't on her for long. Suddenly, everyone began murmuring their take on the last few days, how it had personally traumatized them, and how they were sure things would only get worse. After listening as hard as she could and picking up snippets of information, Judy at last put together what the big controversy of the day was: Maxine was supposedly angry that Diane had heroically "stood up to her" for the evil article Maxine had written. Then last night, Maxine had put everyone at school on notice on Facebook that she would be retaliating today when she brought a gun to school to carry out her own brand of justice.

Judy's heart raced and her head throbbed. She might not have understood Maxine's essay, but she knew Maxine would *never* threaten anyone with a gun or violence of any kind. Just like she had known that Mary would never have told their time travel secret to James O'Grady, even when everyone else had been sure Mary had.

"Maxine would never—" Judy started to say, but stopped when she heard Diane in mid-sentence, responding to a question someone had just asked her about when she had seen Maxine's threatening Facebook posts.

"I didn't even see it right away at first; I was just avoiding homework, as per usual, surfing the web." Diane batted her eyelashes innocently. An alarm went off in Judy's mind. It was just what Diane had said to her on Facebook last night. Facebook. There's no way Maxine even was *on* Facebook! Judy was the only one of her friends using the computer very much. It was all still so strange to them and she knew from her own experience how much the five of them resisted certain things about the future, hoping that if they never made it their own, they could go back to 1955 that much sooner, unsullied by and unattached to the future.

But if Maxine didn't have a Facebook page, who had posted . . . ? Judy's eyes narrowed as she studied Diane Dunkelman. Diane sure didn't look too threatened or afraid of any real danger. She flipped her hair flirtatiously, taking French fries off of Bob's plate and then throwing them right back at him laughingly, even as she spun story after story about how victimized she'd been.

Judy *knew* it: Diane Dunkelman had set up that page to make it look like it was Maxine's. She felt indignation roil in her stomach. At the same moment that she was convinced of what Diane had done, Judy was convinced of what she herself would have to do. She would find a way to prove what Diane had done and exonerate her friend Maxine.

Judy leaned forward as Diane had. "You know what I think?" Judy said, barely above a whisper. Diane, Carla and all the others went quiet again and came closer. "I think Maxine Marshall is jealous of you," Judy said. The words were bitter coming out of her lips and felt like poison on her tongue. But she knew she had just done the best acting job of her life because Diane nodded slowly, her eyes alight with self-congratulatory satisfaction.

Judy almost broke character when she spotted Bev and Ann staring right at her from several tables away. They hadn't heard what she'd said, certainly, but it was enough that she was even sitting with Diane Dunkelman. With all the will-power she had, she kept her eyes on Diane and ignored her friends.

❖   ❖   ❖

Judy kept her eyes forward. She intentionally sat in the front row of Mrs. Fairview's class so that she wouldn't look any of her friends in the face. Her plan wouldn't work if she didn't play this just right. She noticed with a knot in her stomach that Maxine wasn't in fifth period.

Mrs. Fairview took the opportunity to discuss the First Amendment and its implications. Judy watched, enthralled, as Mrs. F became her typical animated self in discussing something historical. Her gestures and expressions were just like they were in 1955; and lit up like this, Mrs. F looked like she hadn't aged a day . . . which got Judy to wondering how it was that Mrs. F had aged when no one else had, except for possibly Aunt Row. As much as she wanted to follow the important points Mrs. F was bringing out in class (especially because she was obviously addressing what was going on with Maxine), Judy's mind wandered to their time travel dilemma. She realized how quickly they had abandoned trying to go back to 1955; but not one of them had a clue as to how to go about doing it.

" . . . does freedom mean no consequences?" Mrs. F was asking. "And is it possible for some citizens to be free if not everyone is free?"

The students murmured and started talking out of turn. This was one class Judy had where all the kids paid attention—partly because Mrs. F didn't allow cell phones in her class and partly because she was fun to listen to when she got riled up.

If not everyone is free. Mrs. Fairview's words replayed themselves in Judy's mind and sparked something. That was exactly it. All five of the girls had to be on the same page to go back to 1955; they couldn't be living their separate lives with their own selfish agendas. They had to work together. Judy was certain that this was true; she wasn't the smartest one in the group, but she knew that much. Her eye caught Mrs. F's as Judy recalled Mrs. F's last words to them in 1955: *Promise that you'll be friends forever.*

It made Judy that much more determined to find out what Diane Dunkelman was up to. She just hoped it wasn't a backwards step that would drive her friends away for good.

At the closing bell, she caught a glimpse of her friends' faces: Mary, Ann, and Bev looked grim.

Judy cast her eyes to the ground and scurried away like the rat they were sure she was.

❖   ❖   ❖

Maxine felt a calm confidence. She knew she was in a lot of trouble, but there was something exhilarating about it. Not that she liked being a troublemaker, exactly . . . but she was standing up for something that she believed in. Dr. King would be proud, she surmised. She was being accused of something she hadn't done. She could kick and scream and make a fuss, or she could stand with the truth. The truth would make her free.

Her parents finally arrived and her confidence faltered. The dull tension that had stretched between Maxine and Principal Jones in his office snapped and the room filled with electricity when John and Gloria Marshall burst in. Maxine had rarely seen her father in offense mode, his voice rich and booming, his gestures dramatic and sweeping. Her mother was quiet for once, but her expression bore her anger and displeasure. At first, Maxine thought her parents' rage was directed at her; but her dad's sharp words to Principal Jones clarified the issue. He wanted to know why his daughter was being singled out when she'd never been in trouble before and what proof they had that she'd been behind the threat.

Seeing her folks so agitated worried Maxine. She was tempted to admit to the crime just so they would go away and leave her at school, but she knew that such a tidy resolution wasn't an option. Principal Jones admitted they were still "gathering proof" pertaining to Maxine's supposed threat, and her dad exclaimed they would be getting a lawyer. Maxine suddenly just wanted to take a nap (which was probably horrifically lazy, she admonished herself, not being able to conceive of Dr. King just wanting to take a nap when he was most needed). Principal Jones's already impatient mood deteriorated and he suggested the three Marshalls leave school during the rest of the investigation and if Maxine was found innocent, it would be considered a day off school; but if guilty . . . .

John Marshall jumped out of the burgundy leather arm chair in front of the principal's desk to protest, but his wife placed a strong hand on his arm. Maxine wanted to say something, apologize for the commotion at the very least, but she found no words to express how she was feeling. And besides that, she didn't trust her voice.

She was grateful they left the office when class was in session and the halls were empty of staring eyes. Waiting for Maxine outside the office door, Mrs. F lingered purposefully. Maxine wanted to embrace her teacher, but imagined her parents would not have approved.

When a tall, blond, overly made-up lady who looked like Diane Dunkelman's much older twin sister came blustering through the school halls as the Marshalls made their way out escorted by Mrs. F, Maxine couldn't help but have a spark of pity for Principal Jones and the pressure he must be under.

"Hey, I think that's . . . . " She gestured toward the lady, who must have been Mrs. Dunkelman on a rampage.

"Just keep walking," Mrs. F smiled pleasantly, steering the Marshalls down a side hallway to veer them off a collision course with Mrs. Dunkelman. When they rounded a corner to head outside, Mrs. F asked Maxine's parents if she could speak to Maxine privately for a moment.

They reluctantly agreed and Mrs. F. took Maxine to a large oak tree on the edge of the school parking lot. They stood under it.

"I remember when this tree was only about ten feet tall," Mrs. F said, gazing at the expansive canopy above her.

"Me, too," Maxine said. Her hands were shaking. She hoped Mrs. F wouldn't notice.

Mrs. F laughed. "Of course you do." She studied Maxine in silence for a moment. She seemed to be trying decide what to say.

"Do you think I should just apologize?" Maxine asked quietly. Her voice quivered and she sounded uncharacteristically vulnerable.

"Whatever would you apologize for?" Mrs. Fairview asked.

"I could just take the blame and it would be over. Principal Jones said they make examples of bullies."

Mrs. Fairview gently touched Maxine's cheek with a motherly affection. "It won't be over just because you take the blame, especially if it's a lie." She sighed. "I have to confess something." She paused, then pressed on, knowing that Maxine's parents were waiting for her. "I've been a lot of . . . *places*, do you understand what I mean?"

Maxine nodded. Mrs. F had been to a lot of different *times*.

"Well, I've always gone to the *past*. So this—this here and now—is as new to me as it is to you. But I can promise you this: it *always* works out. There's always a reason. That's been the one truth that is constant. Never change who you are, because it's who you *are* that's going to get you through this or any mess."

Mrs. Fairview's eyes crinkled into a comforting expression and then she looked at the charm around Maxine's throat, Ann's Star of David.

"It's Ann's," Maxine said.

Mrs. Fairview nodded. "Oh, yes, it always works out." Now she smiled broadly, radiant with hope.

"Thanks for standing by me, Miss Boggs," Maxine said, suppressing a desire to weep.

"It's Mrs. Fairview, sweetheart. And you're welcome; after all, that's what friends are for."

❖   ❖   ❖

"Hey, wait up," James called.

He'd parked himself outside the guys' locker room in hopes of catching Twigler, the elderly school janitor. Sure enough, the old guy rounded the corner with his typical slow gait, pushing a mop in a large bucket on wheels. Twig didn't stop, either assuming James was talking to someone else, or not hearing him at all. James jogged over to him.

"I know you're working," he said, "but can I ask you a question?"

Twig glanced around, surprised at being approached by anyone other than Principal Jones. James only talked to him when he was distributing his little underground newspaper and needed help.

"No, I don't do windows," Twig said brusquely.

James laughed uncomfortably. Twig seemed mad and like he didn't appreciate being disturbed. He worked among hundreds of kids every day, yet he was always alone. James had second thoughts, but at the same time didn't want to miss his last chance. He cleared his throat. Twig kept walking, so James strolled alongside him.

"I, uh, I just heard today that you're retiring."

Twig's response was a snort.

"I guess I always thought you'd be around forever," James said cryptically.

"Is that a question?" Twig muttered.

"Oh, sorry. Uh. I guess what I mean is, I always wanted to interview you for *The Invisible Truth*. You know, to get your story."

"Don't have a story." Twig leaned over to pick up stray papers and candy wrappers in the hallway between the gym and the school building which was lined with lockers. He shoved the trash in his pocket.

"Everyone has a story. Especially you. I looked you up. You were a star football player and you even got drafted to play pro." James echoed Twig in picking up trash but declined cramming it into his own pocket.

"It's not an *interesting* story, then," Twig amended. Two kids raced by, not noticing Twig as they jostled him on their way to the gym. They proved Twig's point: no one was interested in him; he was an old guy and a janitor—*invisible*.

"I also saw that you built a company from the ground up and sold it. I assume you made a lot of money, but here you are working in a school. You act like you want to be left alone, but then you surround yourself with people." James didn't want to be nosy or pushy, but then again, if he was ever going to be an investigative journalist, he'd have to be assertive.

"What do you want from me, kid? Don't you think it's a little creepy to stalk an old man?"

James reddened. Maybe it was a stupid idea after all. "Never mind, I'm sorry to bother—"

"What did you have in mind, a tea party where we dish on all our secrets?" The old dude was getting more crotchety by the second.

"I said never mind."

Twig sighed. "I just don't like people poking around in my business." James realized then that Twig hadn't actually said no.

"You don't have to tell me anything that you don't want to," promised James.

"Fine, but only because I don't mind your writing style."

"You know my writing style? But *The Invisible Truth* is anonymous."

Twig laughed a rusty cackle. "That's what you think." He shook his head, smiling. James didn't appreciate that the smile was at his expense, but at least he'd gotten his interview.

They agreed to meet after Twigler was off work and James was done with track practice. Now that it was set up, James felt apprehensive. Why he was so intrigued by the grizzled guy in the first place, he wasn't sure.

14

Girl for Sale

Marion chewed on her lip. She'd been doing that a lot lately and if she didn't stop, she wouldn't have any lip left. She considered taking up biting her nails again, but her mother would kill her. If they ever saw each other again.

"Uh-oh," Row said, upon seeing the expression on May's face.

"Hush. You don't know what I'm thinking," said May.

"Oh, don't I?" It felt good to tease May; there hadn't been nearly enough laughter since they'd landed back in time. Everyone around May and Row seemed more lighthearted than the two girls, even though the two girls were the ones who knew from the history books that things would turn out for the better—more or less.

They had been sent on an errand by Row's great-great-grandmother, Fiona. Neither of the girls had slept well and they had been practically giddy to get out of the house—and barn. Lachlan had dropped them at the general store to purchase wool yarn and lace and would retrieve them on his way home from the big hardware store in downtown St. Louis. When Fiona had handed Row three crisp dollar bills, Row's and May's eyes had gotten big at how funny the money had looked; Fiona had assumed they hadn't seen that much money at one time before and laughed. "I'll be wanting change, but you can buy yourselves a piece of candy each," she'd said.

But now Row stood with May in the general store teasing her, but she was actually only half-kidding. "Tell me what I'm thinking, then," May said.

"That Lachlan brought us this far and we should find Em."

"So you are a mind-reader."

They browsed through the shelves, oohing and ahhing over the items with funny names: pemmican, which appeared to be buffalo meat flakes; jars of oysters; tins of biscuit mix; and jars of colorful candy, shelved not quite far enough away from the dried fish. Some brands of crackers, vegetables, jellies, condiments, and mincemeat were familiar, but had old-fashioned packaging.

"May, I'm with you, really I am. But I still think we need some sort of a plan—"

May and Row saw the sign on the back wall of the store at the same time and stopped dead.

FOR SALE

A NEGRO GIRL, LIGHT SKIN MULATTO. Healthy, 15 years old. Hard worker, good cook, good ironer, domestic or field. FERTILE/CHILD BEARING FEMALE. SLAVE & offspring for life. Apply TO **CRAWFORD K. DUNKELMAN $400.00**

"Excuse me," May said, turning suddenly to the store clerk who was behind the counter measuring meal from larger burlap bags into smaller canvas ones. "Do you know anything about this"—she nearly choked on the words—"slave girl for sale?"

"Who wants to know?" the man said gruffly.

"My uncle. Lachlan Nolan," Row piped up.

The man laughed a hacking wheeze. "Nolan would no sooner buy a slave from that mudsill Dunkelman than I would swim across the ocean with a barrel of rocks. What are you getting at?"

"He—he needs help, constructing outbuildings with winter coming and all," Row tried again.

"Well, a fifteen-year-old girl ain't gonna help with construction." The man laughed again and Row's cheeks glowed pink.

Now it was May's turn. She was as desperate as Row but tried to not let it show. "It's just that, well, we're fifteen, too. And we know, uh, Mr. Dunkelman. He's a cruel man—"

"That he is," agreed the shopkeeper, for the first time in accord with the girls.

"—and she's an orphan. He's got no right to sell her."

"As you can see, I do not deal in the slave trade. I deal in biscuits, lard, and textiles. You best tell the orphanage. If anything, they'll want some of the sale."

"I think we have a plan: go get her now." May grasped Row's hand and they darted to the front of the store.

But Row stopped suddenly, still holding May's hand and thrusting her wrist toward the shopkeep.

"How much for this watch, sir? It's solid gold and imported from Germany—er, Europe." Row remembered from studying the Great World War and the rise of the Third Reich that that part of the world wasn't the German Empire until 1871. She was quite proud of herself for this quick thinking.

May snatched her hand away from Row with a panicked look in her eye. "No!" she said sternly to Row. May couldn't bear the thought of parting with the watch that certainly must be the only way home to 1945.

"But we've got to help Emily—"

"There's got to be another way, Row, or we—all three of us—will never get back!" They tugged on each other briefly as they argued, but then May gasped, "Oh!"

Judah Jackson passed in front of the store. Without needing to consult one another, the two girls dashed out the tall wooden and glass doors after him. Understanding the importance of not drawing attention to themselves or Judah, May resisted the urge to call out his name and instead made their way toward him through the thin crowd of Victorian-era characters. When they caught up, they kept their voices low.

"Mister . . . Judah," May addressed him as courteously as possible. She wanted to throw her arms around him because he was familiar and most likely had news of Em.

Judah, startled, seemed to take a moment to register who she was.

"I'm sorry if I got you in trouble at all," May pleaded, trying to keep from getting shrill. Her heart raced.

"No trouble, miss," he assured her, but he kept walking without acknowledging her or Row with his body language, except for a slight nod for them to follow.

"That Mr. Dunkelman is selling our friend!" Row burst out uncharacteristically. "Please, you have to help us! He has no right!"

Judah paused only slightly before nodding his head meaningfully toward a Baptist church partway down the block. "Go there," he said almost inaudibly. "An' I was meanin' to bring this to you." He passed a letter discreetly to May that he'd concealed in his shabby pants. She stared at the note until Row snatched it to hide it away, looking around them worriedly. Without a last glance, Judah disappeared down a side street.

At first, May couldn't believe their good luck, running into Judah who had a message for them. Later she would rethink "luck" and acknowledge instead divine intervention. Row tugged May's arm toward the small building with a white steeple and May realized it was the church that she and Emily had hidden behind the morning they had first arrived in 1864. From this angle, she recognized it as the old church several miles from her home that was next door to a gas station.

"Let's get off the street," Row encouraged.

Upon entering the church, the girls immediately felt calmer. A woodburning stove gave off a pleasant heat and homey hearthside smell. The oil lamps along both walls, between the arched windows above the pews, burned a welcoming glow. The girls slid into the second to last pew.

Certain they were alone, Row pulled out the letter and the girls hunched over it, reading it eagerly.

To my friends,

I hope my note finds you well. I miss you. It feels like so much longer than days that I've seen you. It feels like another lifetime. I'm

asking for your help. The man that I work for has a gun. He hit me for wearing squeaky shoes and has threatened to hurt my family. I am so frightened, but I feel brave at the same time, too. I don't know how it's possible, but maybe you understand. I cannot use names in this letter because I don't want to get anyone in trouble, especially the person who is bringing you this letter. But there are people who can help us—me and my family—will you please find them and get us away from this place? Maybe then we can worry about getting back home. I have a horrible, sinking feeling that maybe you went home without me and I don't know what I'll do if that's the case. The man who brought this letter will meet you at a place (he will tell you where) 2 days from now at the same time. Please help. Friends forever.
~E

They finished reading the letter at the same time and Row crushed the letter to her chest. May closed her eyes and bowed her head. Row waited and when May didn't lift her head, Row bowed hers, too.

May didn't know what Row prayed, but May's prayer was a longing without words. She wanted peace and justice and safety for her friends. She didn't know how to go about doing this and reached out with everything she had to hear an answer. This time, she pleaded with God, please don't say no.

"May I help you?" a gentle voice interrupted.

May and Row jumped and stood at attention. Row quickly shoved the letter in the pocket of her skirt.

"You may sit," the man said. His pleasant voice matched his countenance. A colored man with graying hair and kind eyes, he wore a dark suit and the collar of clergy.

"We're sorry to disturb you; we should go anyway. Our ride back home is coming to get us," May said.

"Never mind disturbing me. I think there is always a reason God brings someone in here and it is not always my business why if you do not want to confide in me."

"Our friend is in trouble," Row spoke hastily, cutting to the chase.

May was about to shush Row when she realized this must be the place they were supposed to meet Judah in two days. And maybe this was the place that had the people that could help. May said directly, "Judah Jackson sent us in."

"You know Judah Jackson?" the preacher asked. He sat in the pew in front of the girls, but was turned to face them.

May was about to say that he was the great-grandfather of her best friend, but thought better of it. She nodded instead.

"A lot of folks come to church for help as a last resort," the preacher smiled. "I like to think of God as my first resort."

While Row was pondering how they were to reply to a statement like that, an idea continued to blossom in May's mind. This might be the church and the gentleman pastor that she had read about briefly in school who was associated with the Underground Railroad. In the history books, there was all of one paragraph about the Underground Railroad, but maybe that one paragraph was enough to help them right now. Her heart fluttered and her mouth went dry. She was sitting in front of a real live hero. They would have to say just the right thing, but this could be exactly who they needed. Maybe sitting in front of her was the very reason they had time-traveled!

She knew they would need to speak in some sort of code so as not to implicate the man. May wished suddenly she was more familiar with the Bible so she could quote verses to him that would meaningfully convey her and Row's intention.

"Sir, would you agree that while God is a first resort for help, He also sends helpers to those who are willing but unable to help themselves?"

Row looked at May baffled; why was she choosing now to have a philosophical or theological debate?

"Yes," he said with a slow, warm smile.

"And that maybe those helpers are like conductors on a railroad to freedom?"

Row caught on to May's meaning as she recalled learning about Harriet Tubman, who had led hundreds of slaves to freedom in secret, or underground. May was a genius. Perhaps all that reading and studying that Row often teased May for would pay off. She let May continue to take the lead.

"Some folks say that slavery is a blessing for slaves, providing them food, shelter, and even a religious education." The man tested May.

May couldn't help but think of the devastation the Jews of her day had just endured at the hands of the Nazis. The cost of America waiting too long to go to war was that millions of Jews had been sent to concentration camps (where they also were "fed" and "sheltered").

"Freedom is a God-given blessing," May said fervently. She couldn't spend even the fraction of a second considering what could possibly be right about a person being held against her will as a slave. Evidently Row was thinking along the same lines, because she spoke up, too.

"Where we come from we fight for freedom, even if it means risking our own lives." Row radiated with pride for her brothers, Kell, Orvan, and Wally Jr., and their heroic sacrifice. She was ready to follow in their footsteps.

"Your friend . . . . " The minister urged the girls to provide more information.

"Her name is Emily Jackson and Crawford Dunkelman is selling her. He has no right to her. Not just because . . . he just can't . . . she must . . . we have to . . . . "

"You came to the right place," the minister assured them, so quietly they almost didn't hear him.

❖   ❖   ❖

It wasn't the ideal time to escape, and in fact the Quaker, the minister, and the other mystery underground railroad conductor who helped May and Row with the plan advised against the timing. The winter conditions were too harsh and they wouldn't be fleeing under the total darkness of a new moon, but Emily was going to the auction block in two days. There was no one else here who knew her or would challenge Dunkelman's right to sell her.

May pulled the scratchy wool blanket closer. But she knew it wouldn't help; it wasn't the chilly November air that kept her shivering. It was knowing that when the clock struck midnight, she would risk everything for her friend. While she lay in bed in the Nolans' well-appointed mansion, not daring to think of missing a Thanksgiving feast back home with her family, her friend miles away probably counted the moments to her escape from a cruel slave master.

Normally, May would not have been so brave; but tonight she would do anything for Emily. It had been her own fault, of that May was certain. The fact that Row hadn't tried to talk her out of it had only confirmed that May was indeed to blame. She didn't know if her actions tonight might rewrite history, might even rewrite Emily right out of her life; but she did know that Crawford Dunkelman had a gun—and knew how to shoot it.

And she didn't know how three girls, three slaves, and a slave master's grand-baby—Em's great-grandfather—were going to cross the Mississippi River in the middle of the night . . . she just knew they had to try.

With that, May swung her feet out of bed and folded the blanket. It had felt strange staying in what would be Wally's —her first love's —room several decades into the future and she was eager to leave behind the sad thought that Wally didn't yet exist in the past or anymore in the future. She was already dressed, even with her button-up shoes on. As the dark leather on the top of one of them caught a ray of moonlight, she thought with dread of her friend being beaten for wearing squeaky shoes, and May's courage screwed up. She tore the sleeping cap from her hair, shoved it under her pillow, and marched with silent resolve to retrieve Row. But Row was waiting outside of May's door. Silently, May embraced Row. The thought of trying to do this without her was more than May could bear.

Perhaps Row felt the same because she hugged her friend back with the same intensity.

After May had slipped out of bed with her heart pounding loudly enough, she was sure, to wake all of the Confederate army on both sides of the Mason-Dixon line, Row and May tiptoed carefully through the hallway so as not to wake the baby or Lachlan and Fiona. As far as the minister knew, Lachlan and Fiona were the abolitionists funding this rescue mission and May was just a go-between communicating plans that she knew nothing about. But Row and May had studied carefully every communication and made a few of their own on behalf of Lachlan and Fiona. The girls knew that no matter how opposed to slavery Lachlan and Fiona were, they would never allow two fifteen-year-old girls to participate in something so dangerous, which was why Lachlan and Fiona knew nothing of that night's plan to escort Emily and her friends across the river to safety.

As the two crept onto the side porch, the night sky a blotchy, tarnished pewter, they were met by Finigan, his tail wagging so hard with pleasure at seeing Row that his whole body wiggled. His breath came out in silvery puffs hovering in the bitter night air.

"No," Row whispered as quietly and forcefully as she could at the dog. "Go back to the barn, Finigan!" Even though she knew it couldn't possibly be her dog, her 1945 Finigan—no matter how identical they seemed—she couldn't help but feel the same connection.

"Let's keep going," May insisted in a stage whisper, wishing she had the white rabbit fur muff her dad had gotten her last Christmas. She squinted her eyes against the sharp and frigid darkness. It was going to be a long, cold night.

They quickly made their way to edge of the Nolan property, but still Finigan was at Row's heel.

"Do something," May said about their eager admirer.

"He won't go. Maybe he'll turn back the further away from home we get," Row said, pushing Finigan reluctantly away.

Row and May scampered along the side of the road, finding cover in trees, shrubs, or big structures along the way. May felt heavy with anxiety and dread, yet she knew this was the easiest part of their journey.

First, they were to meet Emily, Gin, Eliza, Judah, and baby Noah in the cellar at the back of the church, and then they were to get directions to a safe house, where they would descend to the cellar to a cave that would take them under the city to the north toward a landing. A skiff would be waiting there. They would take the skiff across the Mississippi to Illinois and they would stay during the day at another safe house. After further instructions, they'd begin the trek again the next night to head further north. It would take months to get to Canada and certain safety. Sadly, Eliza and Judah would be leaving many relatives behind, including their young girl, Violet. They feared that she would not survive the journey and could not even say goodbye, in case she let on that they were leaving.

The part that frightened May more than the possibility of being hunted down, found, and punished was that they might succeed and actually escape. The further they got from Row's house, where they had time traveled, the less hope May felt there would be of getting home again. They could be trapped in this uncivilized era, away from her parents and classmates and even old Theo, her huge, irascible black cat. She had purposefully not tried to find her neighborhood, depressed by the knowledge that where her house stood in 1945 would now be an empty field.

"We only have five hours to meet Em, Judah, Eliza, and Gin at the church, get to the river and cross it. Then it will be daybreak and if we're not in the safe house, we'll be discovered for sure," May said as she and Row ran together. She was calculating the unlikelihood of success; it was three miles to the church and another ten to the river. The river itself was a torrent of dark, muddy, deadly currents. It was mysterious and unpredictable, and May couldn't help but think of Huck Finn and Jim on their raft floating inadvertently right toward the South. Though her torso began to warm up with the exercise of running, she found herself shivering. On top of the distance they needed to cover, they had to remain undetected: since 1861, St. Louis had been under martial law, Lachlan reminded them several times.

"I know it, May," huffed Row in response to May's concerns. "But we can't think of all that. We have to just keep moving one step at a time."

Finigan kept pace with them and looked like he had no intention of turning back.

They heard rustling in a hedge up ahead and stopped dead in their tracks. Finigan grumbled, at first almost beneath his breath, but then it evolved into a threatening growl. He advanced slowly, one paw placed purposefully in front of the other.

"No!" breathed Row. "Fin, come back right now."

Finigan ignored her and suddenly leaped forward. A snarling hurricane of aggression broke out and Row and May jumped behind a tree, trying to make out just what it was Finigan was attacking. A yelp echoed through the night and a four-legged figure slunk away. Finigan trotted back to May and Row with proud satisfaction. He nudged Row's hand and then they moved forward more tentatively, hearts beating wildly.

"I guess that answers that question. Fin comes with us," May said, catching her breath. As they picked up the pace again, May looked over and saw the defeated husky black dog sitting at the side of the road with his head hung low. He didn't bark or so much as raise his eyes in the direction of Finigan, Row, and May.

"Good boy," Row whispered to Fin.

The girls quickly learned to watch Finigan's subtle reactions. When he slowed, they slowed and when he dashed ahead, they tried to keep up. While May's senses were on high alert, at the same time her mind wandered. First, she tried to imagine a Thanksgiving meal with her family back home in 1945, celebrating the end of the war and being together, making plans to see her grandparents and cousins at Christmas in Ohio; but it didn't make her feel better, it actually slowed her pace and made her heart hurt. She forced herself to consider something else instead.

She thought of her neighbors, the Hayashis.

Mr. and Mrs. Hayashi had twin boys two years older than May and a daughter a year younger than her. The Hayashis had met and fallen in love when Mr. Hayashi had moved to the States when he was a little boy and married when they were still fairly young. Mrs. Hayashi's parents had been born in America. Time and again, May's mother said they couldn't have asked for better neighbors. The Hayashis were quiet, respectful, and clean, and could be relied upon to borrow a cup of rationed sugar at any time. The daughter, Renge, whom they called "Lily" in English, and May played together sometimes and Lily's brothers helped Mr. Boggs around the yard whenever there was a big project.

When Pearl Harbor was attacked by the Japanese on December 7, 1941, the Hayashis had been the last people on May's mind. But the Hayashis had cut off communication and kept the curtains in their house closed. Within months, they'd been given forty-eight hours to pack what they could carry because they were being "relocated."

When May had asked her dad, "Are they going back to their country?"

He had said gruffly, "This is their country, Marion."

May hadn't even known that her dad had a gun until the Hayashis were getting ready to move to a camp in Arkansas. People had gathered outside the Hayashis' home. Some were curious and just gawking, others waited to take whatever the Hayashis left behind. One moment, Mr. Hayashi had been a respected dentist and the next, many of his neighbors and patients had treated him like a dangerous criminal.

Normally a happy-go-lucky guy, May's father had transformed into a raging tower of indignation. For months after the Hayashis had gone, May had heard her father bellowing in her parents' room every night. May had known he wasn't yelling at her mom, but it had still frightened her. She hadn't been used to that side of him.

When a letter had come from Mr. Hayashi requesting May's father vouch for Mr. Hayashi's status as a loyal American, Mrs. Boggs had begged her husband "not to get involved." The two had gone round and round about it and May wished she could have come to her father's and the Hayashi family's defense.

One spring day, as the daffodils had just popped open their cheerful yellow faces, when May got home from school, her mother was waiting by the door in her nicest hat, coat, and gloves. "I want you to come with me when I do this," was the only thing she had said in explanation. She'd had a letter in her hand.

They had walked together the several blocks to the post office in silence. Then, Mrs. Boggs had held up the envelope for May to see. It was addressed to the internment camp where the Hayashis were living in Jerome, Arkansas. Before placing it into the outgoing slot, May's mom had said, "Honey, I'm proud to be an American; but sometimes it makes me sad, too."

May had given her mom a hug before Mrs. Boggs released the letter into the mailbox.

That had been the last of the fighting between her parents and at dinner that night, May had noticed her father brushing her mom's cheek gently, touching her hair, squeezing her hand at every opportunity.

A couple of years later, last year in 1944, before the war was even over, the Hayashis had returned to their home next door. But they had still kept their curtains closed and the one time May had gone over to borrow a cup of sugar—a pretext to just say hi and welcome back to Lily—they hadn't even answered the door. Within months, they had moved away. Dr. Hayashi's practice had been ruined and the family had no longer felt a connection to the community.

May had never been so proud of her parents and so ashamed of her country (until now). Thinking of the effort her parents had made on behalf of the Hayashis, even if it had been a small gesture in the scheme of things, kept May moving forward on this bleak winter night to help Emily and her family. May realized, though, that she could not proceed with a heart divided—scared of succeeding and being further from the place where they had time traveled, and wanting to succeed and be further away from a place where slavery was legal. It was all or nothing. The Hayashis hadn't been the same when they'd come home and for Emily and her group, there was no such thing as coming home. The only option was escape.

"How much further?" Row whispered as the two of them and the dog came to an intersection. On one side was an open field in front of big woods; on the other, a row of homes, only one of which had a gaslight on, casting an eerily pale green glow on the rest of the street. Down the block was a row of businesses: a bank, a lumber yard, a tavern. The night was mostly quiet with its residents tucked under layers of wool blankets. Who would be out at this hour in these temperatures, after all? May's nose and tops of her ears burned with cold.

May paused at the corner, under the cover of a large bitternut hickory tree whose leaves now crunched under their feet in a frail, frosty kaleidoscope. Finigan came to a stop and sat at May's feet, leaning ever so slightly against May's leg, warming it. May had never considered herself a dog person where pets were concerned, but Finigan and Finigan's twin were quickly changing her mind.

"Don't tell me we're lost," Row said, looking around frantically.

"We're not lost. I don't think so. I've never made this trek at night," May said, doubt creeping into her voice. In the daytime, when she'd first headed this direction with Emily, she had followed the activity and the visible pollution from the steamboats on the Mississippi and headed toward the city. But now in the dark, and without the city lights and familiar landmarks of 1945 to serve as a beacon, May was growing concerned. She tried to imagine what turn they had taken when they'd first come upon Eliza, Noah, and Judah on the street with the large abusive white man. If only there were enough moonlight, and they could get to higher ground to spot the steeple or the smokestacks of the steamboats on the river, or the river itself. Then she remembered the railroad; they just needed to stay close to the railroad and head east. She let out a breath of relief.

"Soldiers!" Row hissed suddenly and Finigan stood at attention.

May heard it too: clattering, loud scuffling, and men's agitated voices. Even as they tried to determine which direction the commotion came from, May's mind raced, thinking of where they could hide. The field across the street offered no options, so she grabbed Row's collar and they leapt behind a shrub in front of the row homes.

"Fin!" cried Row. For once, the dog didn't run ahead to confront the danger, but obediently scurried with them to squat behind the prickly holly bushes. In barely a moment, it was clear where the stir was coming from: eight white men with guns and flaming torches approached from the direction May and Row were headed. They appeared to be kicking and tossing a large, heavy bag between them, yelling obscenities and rousing the whole town.

Now Finigan couldn't help but growl, but Row kept a tight grasp on his ruff. These were not people whose attention they wanted.

Just when May was about to whisper to Row, "What are they throwing around?" she realized with a flicker of one of the torches that it was not a what, but a who.

Judah Jackson was not waiting for them at the church. He had been caught.

15

Friends and Faux

James was nervous and he wasn't sure why. He'd interviewed plenty of people, including the police chief and even the mayor (but those had been official business for the school newspaper). Now, getting ready to meet Twigler, the school janitor, James felt uneasy; perhaps it was a premonition that through talking to Twig, James would discover something that he wished he didn't know.

He was also acutely aware of feeling unsettled about Mary. There was a conversation they needed to have if he wanted to salvage their friendship. And he did want to. But he also wished it could be simple and she could just trust him. Of course, that probably wouldn't have been an issue if he hadn't been so public with his thoughts about Ann.

Summer weather was in full swing, even as school was still in session for another restless week and a half. Students and teachers alike seemed at once agitated, impatient, and carefree in a celebratory way, which made for a volatile atmosphere. It all added fuel to the controversy started by Maxine's essay. James didn't know how that would end; if Maxine outed him as the editor of the underground paper, he could be in trouble. He was less concerned about getting reprimanded and more concerned about his fellow students, influential kids like Bob Jenkins and Diane Dunkelman, who were eager to make a spectacle of Maxine. One moment, the students all seemed lazy and careless; and the next, they were outraged by something they couldn't articulate the meaning of.

It all made James wish he belonged to another generation. Which brought the uneasy lump in his throat back and reminded him of Twig. James leaned against the back wall of the gym, sweat forming a glistening band across his forehead even though he leaned into the shade. He wondered why he had bothered showering after track practice. They had one more meet on Saturday and then it was up to him to be self-disciplined enough to train during the summer in this horrific heat.

"You mind walking with me?"

James jumped slightly as Twig came from the murky shadows of the school building behind him.

"Sure. I mean, no. I don't mind." James fumbled with his tiny digital recorder. "Do you mind if I record—?"

Twig waved his bony hand at James and James didn't know if he was waving away James's need to ask, or waving away the idea of recording their conversation. James quickly turned the recorder on anyway but tucked it into his pocket. Who knew what the recording would come out like, but he didn't want to needle Twig by holding it out in the open.

"So, are you from St. Louis originally?" James asked. The two walked away from the parking lot, where Twigler's car was probably parked, and toward the baseball field. There, James spotted some of his friends, like Duncan Marsalis and Conrad Marshall, along with the Jenkins kids—Bob and Bev—all toughing it out in the heat getting ready for their next playoff game. Watching practice from the stands were Diane Dunkelman, freshly showered from softball practice, and—James found this curious—Judy White.

"Born and raised," Twig answered James.

"And what was your childhood like?" James was off his game. What a horrible question. How was Twig supposed to answer that, with some trite adjective: *nice, interesting, good*? He was needing to get Twig warmed up before he asked what he really wanted to know: about the top-secret research Twig's company had been contracted to do for the US government.

Twig laughed his gruff laugh, which sounded more like a noise mocking James for his ridiculous question. "It was interesting," Twig responded, which was just as banal an answer as James deserved.

"Did you go to school here?"

"I did. Couldn't wait to get out of this town, go to a big city like New York or Chicago, but here I am."

"Why did you stay?" James asked. His nerves calmed. They were getting on the right track.

"Never thought I'd see the day where a girl plays for the boys' team," said Twig, catching a glimpse of Bev who was running toward them to field a ball. After smoothly hurling the ball to her brother, Bev gave James a little wave and trotted back to her position.

"She's pretty good," James said.

"Helps to have brothers."

"Helps to have talent," James rebutted, but then wondered if he came across as discourteous to Twig. Twig just laughed in consent. "So why did you hang around here after all?" James refocused.

"When I went to school here, we didn't have girls' teams. Some of the girls liked to play field hockey for fun after school, but most of the girls took dancing lessons or went home to help their families. They had dads and brothers at war and moms working in the factories."

"Did you? Have a dad or brothers at war or a mom working in the factory?"

Twig looked at James like he had two heads. "No."

Suddenly, Twig's words dawned on James belatedly. "Wait, you went to school . . . *here*? Did you know my aunt, Rowena Nolan?"

Twig paused before launching into a tirade. "See, now here's what drives me nutty about you kids. Here's a trash can and not two feet away is a pile of rubbish!" Once again, Twig disregarded James's question and found a new focus. He leaned over with a groan and picked up a half-filled-with-soda paper cup and a crumpled fast food bag and tossed them in the garbage. They'd made their way to the front of the school by this point and James wondered if they were just going to lap the school in this unbearable heat while Twig ignored every question James asked.

Feeling like he had nothing to lose, James challenged, "So when you were my age, you were never careless or carefree?"

Twig was quiet for a moment like he hadn't heard James and then he chuckled. "I was pretty careless. I wouldn't say carefree, though. Few of us were. Least of all your aunt." He whistled. "She was a pretty one, that Row."

Now James was quiet, yearning for Twig to keep talking.

"Being family, you probably already know she lost three brothers to the war and her mother killed herself shortly there-after."

"Suicide?" James blurted. He hadn't heard it put that way whenever his mom, who was Aunt Row's stepsister, had talked about the family.

"Some such. Same thing. But that Row . . . she just kept marching right on with her head held high." He stopped walking and talking, ran the back of his hand across his damp forehead. "Didn't mean to talk about her. I guess you have the answer to two questions, now."

James didn't know which two questions Twig was referring to, but before he could clarify, Twig wrapped up the interview with the excuse that he was an old man and it was too hot to be wandering around outside in the sun (as if it had been James's idea).

Twig said good-bye abruptly without giving James a chance to schedule another meeting.

With a heavy sigh, James went to his car and started the engine to get the AC blowing. Then he took the recorder out to erase what was probably all static anyway. He was still wondering what two questions Twig had answered when he heard one of them on his recorder: "Why did you hang around here after all?"

She was a pretty one, that Row . . . she just kept marching right on with her head held high.

He put the car in gear and headed to his aunt's house.

❖   ❖   ❖

"She's not *that* great of a player," sneered Diane Dunkelman.

Judy had noticed that Diane spent more time watching Bev on the field than Bob, whom they were supposedly at practice to watch. Diane had come from her own softball practice. Her team had one more game and their season would be over if they lost. Maybe that, in part, accounted for her bad mood.

Judy decided to keep her mouth shut about Bev. As much as she wanted to be in Diane's good graces, she couldn't choke out one more fake insult about her friends, even to justify the ends. Instead, Judy heard herself say ever so sweetly, "When are you and Bob going to make it official?" She knew this would rankle Diane because she and Bob still weren't "Facebook official," a fact that was a beacon of hope for Judy.

"We have all summer to make it official," huffed Diane, fanning herself in the heat.

Judy was so ready to be done with Diane and be back with her real friends and it had only been a day. She just wanted to hear Diane admit that she had set up Maxine's page on the Internet. "I heard Maxine got suspended," Judy said, hoping to open up the subject.

"Yeah, for like, a *day*. Is that what you do with a terrorist? Slap her on the wrist and say you get a day off of school? Epic fail."

Judy's jaw clenched. Hearing Diane refer to Maxine as a terrorist was more than she could take. *Acting,* she reminded herself. *What would Marilyn Monroe or Natalie Wood do? They would stay in character.*

"Your hair is so cute up like that," Judy said. Now she didn't want to be anywhere near the topic of her friends.

Diane flipped her pony tail. "Aw, you're the sweetest. Hey, do you want to come over to my place after this? I told my mom about how you dress and she can't even believe it."

Judy said, "Sure," while not feeling sure and then looked out at the field at Bev and Bob. She adored them both and hoped that this little scheme of hers would get them back in her life. In the meantime, it was torture. She'd never felt so . . . unlike herself. Having Bev shoot her dirty looks wasn't helping. "Do you want to go now?" Judy asked.

Within minutes, Diane's mom had responded to Diane's text demanding a ride home. Judy thought she had arrived in record time, but Diane said, "Way to make us wait forever in the hot sun, Mom," as she climbed in the front seat of the huge SUV.

Judy had never ridden in a car so big. Mrs. Dunkelman directed Judy to sit in the back and buckle up. With the A/C blasting and the music that Diane had turned on blaring, Judy watched her "old" neighborhood slide by through the dark tinted windows of the Dunkelmans' car. Nostalgia and loneliness cramped her heart. She felt so far from normal, she didn't know if she'd recognize it when she saw it. This couldn't be the reason they had time-traveled. It couldn't possibly come down to her denying her friends and buddying up with bad news Diane Dunkelman. Her plan had to work, it just had to. So instead of feeling sorry for herself, she committed to redoubling her efforts.

Once at the Dunkelmans' huge house, which Judy was certain could be considered a mansion, Diane climbed out of the front seat and told her mom to observe Judy in full view. At the garage door going into the house, Mrs. Dunkelman turned and giggled as she glanced at Judy.

"You're so right, Di! A blast from the past."

When Judy turned red and seemed embarrassed, Diane said to her, "Oh, come on, you can't expect to dress like that and not have people *ogle* you."

Says the girl whose tiny shirt doesn't cover her stomach, thought Judy, but she made a great effort to shrug good-naturedly.

Once in the house, Judy tried to disguise her awe at the scale of the place: tall ceilings, oversized furniture, towering windows that looked onto neighbors' backyards. Past the kitchen in an expansive family room sat Diane's little brother and his friend, Alex Branislav.

"Did you bring snacks?" Franco hollered at his mom, not turning his head from the video game he and Alex were playing. Alex, however, looked up and spotted Judy. His brows knit together in a questioning expression and Judy simply put her finger to her mouth, hoping he'd clam up and not bring his big sister, Ann, into a conversation.

"There's plenty of food in the pantry," sighed Mrs. Dunkelman.

"Yeah, but nothing I like," muttered Franco as his character on the screen exploded into a disgusting mess.

Alex tore his eyes from Judy and turned his attention to his move in the game, but his heart didn't seem in it.

"Let's get out of here. I gotta text Carla," sighed Diane, heading toward the front of the house. Judy followed. A massive curved staircase with an ornate balustrade and decorative iron spindles led from the front door to the second level of the house and Diane ascended it, with Judy behind her.

Judy couldn't help but compliment Diane on her home.

"Yeah, my mom got to keep the house and kids. Dad lives in a condo," Diane said laughingly, but Judy sensed a sensitivity there.

"Sorry," Judy said about the Dunkelmans' divorce.

"I'm not. I have a huge room!" Diane simpered.

At the end of a long hall, they turned and walked through a set of double doors. As Diane had indicated, her room was huge. But Judy didn't notice the size of it, or the fact that it was professionally decorated in sumptuous lavender silks and had its own bathroom and balcony; what she noticed was the laptop sitting on Diane's desk. *Eureka!* thought Judy, who couldn't wait to prove that Diane had set up a phony account in Maxine's name.

Diane threw herself onto her bed and immediately got out her phone to start texting. Judy stood, holding her books from school lamely, and stared at the computer twelve feet away. She could feel it pulling her like a magnet.

"Can I check my Facebook?" Judy asked.

"I don't care," Diane said, already done with having a guest.

As Judy approached the desk, however, Diane suddenly leapt off the bed and intercepted the computer. "Let me just make sure I'm logged off," she said. She grabbed the laptop, turning it away from Judy. After a brief moment, she smiled sweetly. "All yours."

Diane sat on the bed, watching Judy. "Hey, do you want a snack?"

Judy considered echoing Diane's flippant, "I don't care," but decided to be polite instead. "That would be cool, thanks."

As soon as Diane left the room, Judy realized she didn't know enough about computers to see if Diane had set up the account.

For the time being, she thought she'd at least go to the site and sign herself in, but she was surprised when Diane's account was already logged in. Didn't she just say she had logged herself *out*? Judy looked at the doors to Diane's room. It would be at least a few minutes before Diane returned . . . maybe Judy could just poke around on Diane's page?

Then a new update came across the screen:

Maxine Marshall: Fooled everybody and got away with it! lol - lovin life.

How had Diane just done that? Judy knew it had to be Diane. Maxine would never talk like that, much less think like that.

A few minutes later, Diane re-entered the room with two cans of diet soda and a bag of potato chips. Judy fumbled on the computer, not having a clear plan as to if she should still be on Diane's page.

"Are you on my account?" Diane said, acting shocked and offended. *If I am that bad of an actress*, Judy thought, *I should stick to learning better computer skills.*

Before Judy could mock-apologize, Diane had grabbed the computer and gasped dramatically. "This is horrible! Look what she's posted now!"

Judy put on an innocent expression. "Who?"

"Maxine Marshall!" Diane shoved the computer toward Judy. Diane's lower lip quivered and Judy nearly burst out laughing. Diane had nerves of steel and a heart of stone; if Maxine had really posted something like that, Diane Dunkelman would have been hopping mad, not on the verge of tears.

"You should tell your mom," Judy advised, still wondering how Diane had managed to post the bulletin in question. "And she should call Maxine's parents." Judy prayed Maxine was with one or both of her parents and so be proved innocent.

"You're right, I'm going to right now." Diane slapped the laptop closed and took it with her. When Judy got up to follow, Diane said, "This will just take a minute. I'll be right back."

Judy went and sat gingerly on Diane's bed. Diane's bed was bigger than Judy's mom's bed. Of course, now that she thought about it, Diane's suite was nearly the size of Bitsy's living room, kitchen, and dining room combined. She jumped when Alex appeared at the door.

"Can you walk me home? I'm supposed to be back for dinner and my mom doesn't like me to walk by myself, even though I'm eleven."

"Well, I—I don't know when I'm headed home myself," Judy said, wanting to wrap up her sting in this visit, but not sure what her next move was.

"If you walk me home, I can tell you about how Diane was on Franco's computer downstairs a minute ago, on my sister's friend's page."

"Let me just get my books and I'll come with you," Judy said.

16

If it's Broke, Fix it

Dear Diary,   May 26

I am a liar.

I have been saying over and over again to myself that I don't care that James O'Grady likes Ann. I have been saying that I don't like him anyway. I have been saying that he is a jerk for liking us both.

But the truth is, Diary, I do care. He convinced me that I might have something to give. And while I've been mulling over these things as if nothing else matters, we are still stuck in the future. And here where/when we are, Maxine is in big trouble for what she wrote about civil rights. She found her voice and the least I can do is stand with her and raise mine; she quotes a leader named Dr. King who said, "We will have to repent in this generation not merely for the vitriolic words and actions of the bad people, but for the appalling silence of the good people." I will have to repent for my "appalling silence." Maybe Mrs. F doesn't have the answers, but she trusts us—me—to find them. No more being a drag, I'm going to fight for my friends.

　　Always,
　　Mary

Dear Diary,　　　　　May 26

　　I did it, I did it, I did it! I found out that Diane Dunkelman was behind the fake Maxine page that sent the school into a tizzy. Well, the article sent the school into a tizzy, but that Internet page got Maxine suspended. I went to Diane Dunkelman's house after school. At first I thought it was cool to be invited to the popular girl's house (more like mansion. You should see her pad!), but when I was there, all I did was miss my friends. I thought Diane was just mean to people she felt threatened by, but it turns out she's mean even to her friends. Ann's brother Alex was there and he helped me crack the case! I walked him home and he explained to me how he saw Diane on the computer updating "Maxine's" page. Diane didn't think Alex was watching because she thinks he's just a stupid kid. But walking home with him made me wish I had a little brother, especially a cool one like Ann's.

When we got to his house, I saw Ann. At first she was real frosted to see me because I've been acting like Diane's friend. But Alex explained what I was doing and what we discovered. Then Ann got really excited and gave me a big hug and started crying and saying that she missed me and that we have to tell the principal the first thing in the morning at school.

It was the first time I'd been to her house. It was tiny compared to Diane's. But Ann's heart is bigger than Diane's ever will be and Ann has more talent and kindness and intelligence in her pinky finger than Diane has in her whole mansion.

Now I hope Maxine will forgive me and we can go back to normal.

Judy White ~~Jenkins~~

Wednesday, May 26 –

You can be all alone in a crowded room. Maybe we all have to learn to not depend on anyone else. I think that is a sad way to go. Or maybe it's not about depending on everyone else, but being someone everyone can depend on. Diane Dunkelman has accused me of things that make no sense at all. At first even my own parents weren't sure if I was lying, but they know me better than that. Ann knows me better than that, too. But Judy has become friends with DD and I can't understand why. 1955 wasn't so great and the future's not much better. It's time for me to make my own way and if that way is the way my friends are going, I will be delighted. But if I have to walk alone, I will put a smile on my face and never look back.

Maxine

Two more days until districts. I can't wait! Bob is feeling better from his blow to the head in our last game and Coach has me slated as shortstop. After this game, it's on to State. I have a good feeling that we can go all the way! Maxine suspended from school for a day. I don't know how to help. Oh, and Conrad Marshall can sure be a real jerk.
- Bev

Dear Irina,   26 May

   I know I can have a video call with you or email you, but I miss putting pen to paper; it helps me sort out my thoughts better. I've started another painting. It's of lilacs - yes, again! The other painting I did was a view of the lilacs through our fence. I got to thinking, that's really a painting of a fence. But what about the view of the lilacs from the other side of the fence? Then the fence is in the past, behind, and the lilacs are free. That is a different view than I am used to: the other side of the fence.

   I hope that someday you will get to meet my friends,

especially Maxine. She wrote an essay that has caused quite a stir. My favorite line from it is, "If we stumble on the way to peace, we can still steady ourselves and find the way. But there is no stumbling where there are no steps forward . . . ." She is such a good writer! I hope that someday I can be half as good a painter.

That terrible girl I've mentioned to you, Diane Dunkelman, has gotten Maxine into some trouble, supposedly over Maxine's essay. But we have a plan to straighten it all out. I'm sure in my next letter, I'll be writing you through tears of joy and victory and not sadness and frustration. At least there is hope . . . and if I stumble, I know that at least I am moving forward.

Your Cousin Always,

~Ann

Mary stood wringing her hands on Aunt Row's porch. Her stomach was in knots and her nerves were frayed. She wanted to talk to James in person and hoped he'd be at Aunt Row's, or that Aunt Row could tell Mary where he was. Before she asked the big favor of him to help her friends, she knew she owed him an apology for how she had treated him. Even if she didn't like what he'd written, she should at least let him explain himself before cutting him out, the way the Fifties Chix had done to

Maxine. Mary didn't know if the apology or begging the favor was making her more nervous, so when it took Aunt Row longer than usual to answer the door, Mary was tempted to turn and make a run for it.

But sure enough . . . .

"Mary! I—didn't expect to see you here," James said, opening the door. He didn't seem angry. In fact, he seemed flushed and excited. Mary had forgotten—or had spent a lot of effort trying to forget—his crooked smile and his kind eyes. Any ambivalence she'd had toward apologizing dissolved instantly.

"I came to find you," Mary said.

"I need to talk to you, too," James said in a rush. He lowered his voice. "I discovered some things that I think you should—"

Aunt Row's voice came from within the house. "Who is it, Jimmy?"

"It's Mary," he called back to her.

"Don't go spilling the beans—"

"Aunt Row, she has to know."

Aunt Row appeared at the door. Her friendly face and youthful features were a welcome sight to Mary. She'd always seemed like a good-natured lady and Mary liked her, even if only because she was Mrs. Fairview's best friend and James's aunt. "Hello, Mary," she welcomed. To James, she said, "Just be wise and use discretion. This isn't mine to tell." She gave him a meaningful look, shook her head in resignation, and kissed the side of his head. Then Aunt Row dismissed herself and went upstairs, leaving James and Mary alone at the front door.

James invited Mary in and they went to the kitchen. Mary remembered her first visit there, when they had been hoping to find Mrs. Fairview. It felt like ages ago, but it had been only last week. The answers Mary and her friends were seeking didn't feel any closer, and 1955 felt even further away. Mary hadn't even been able to find out where Mrs. Fairview had been when she'd disappeared and the girls had come to Row's house seeking her.

"Aunt Row just made some lemonade," James said, pulling out two mismatched glasses.

"I need to say something," Mary said, mustering up her courage.

"Can I go first? There's a lot to say, but I just wanted to give you a lesson in literature before we go any further."

Confounded, Mary agreed.

"Poetry, as I'm sure you know, is full of symbols." James put on his best impression of a stuffy English professor and Mary had to smile. "Take for example, this line: *deeper currents leave no trail*. The imagery is that of deeper currents, sure, but more importantly, we are left with the sense that they leave *no trail*." He paused and returned to his normal voice. "Do you see what I mean?"

"I think so." Mary couldn't have stopped smiling if she wanted to.

"I shouldn't have published something that could have hurt your feelings. I wasn't thinking that it would or could . . . . "

"Of course you can write about your feelings, just as much as Maxine can." Mary had hardly accepted James's apology before launching into her idea. "Which is one of the things I wanted to talk to you about. I know your paper is anonymous—"

"That's debatable," James chuckled.

"—but I wondered if you'd be willing to publish a paper 'above ground,' that's not anonymous. I want to write an essay supporting Maxine and I'll bet we can get the girls to write something, as well."

"It's brilliant, Mary! We could call it . . . *The Visible Truth*! I'll write something, too."

"Mightn't it blow your cover for the other paper?"

"If we get a whole group of kids to write, it'll help; but I don't care if my role as editor is exposed if it helps Maxine."

Mary was so thrilled with their project, she entirely forgot the apology she'd prepared; and she *almost* forgot James's words to Row when Mary had arrived, *"Aunt Row, she has to know."*

"What is it Aunt Row doesn't want you to tell me?" she asked.

James filled the glasses with ice and lemonade and carried them to the big glossy farmhouse table under the windows. Golden light surged through and warmed the kitchen, making blinding reflections on the tabletop and causing Mary to see spots wherever she looked. "You need to be sitting when I tell you this," James said.

Mary sat obediently, her heart in her throat. She wasn't sure that she could swallow very well with how she was feeling, but she still took a sip of lemonade and was grateful for the refreshment.

James sat at the head of the table, around the corner from Mary. "Do you know Twigler?"

Mary thought for a moment. "The custodian?"

James snickered; Twig probably thought no one knew him. "Yep, that's him. Well, he's always—intrigued me, I guess you could say. He helps with *The Invisible Truth*, you know, helps me place it around the school. I just found out that he's retiring this year—"

"—like Miss Boggs!" Mary inadvertently interrupted. "I mean, Mrs. F!"

James smiled. "I knew who you meant. And yeah, exactly like Mrs. F. In fact, he went to school with Mrs. F and Aunt Row."

Things started to click in Mary's mind like a roller coaster ascending a steep track. She tried to make sense of the puzzle pieces. "For the sake of argument, let's say it's 1955."

"Mary," James said, hoping she would stop the hypothetical *for the sake of argument* bit.

She allowed herself a peek at James and sighed. "OK, when I was in 1955 at this age, was he the custodian like he is now—the same age he is now?"

"That's just it. He went to *school* with Row and Mrs. F—Miss Boggs, then—and went to college and played football. He got drafted to play pro ball, but quit to start his own company doing government contract work." James's eyes were big.

Mary wasn't following, but her heart was pumping too much blood for her to breathe normally. She took another sip of lemonade, the ice rattling in the glass.

"Evidently, Miss Boggs had a watch that broke and Aunt Row took it to Twig's foster dad's shop to repair. Twig worked at the shop and when he came across the watch to fix it, there was something extraordinary enough about the watch that he quit everything he was doing and started a company doing government contracting." James paused meaningfully. "Research and development for *time travel*."

Even though Mary didn't have any lemonade in her mouth, she choked. "A watch of Miss Boggs's?" Now her eyes got big. "Is it the fancy gold one she always wears?" Mary jumped from her chair, bumping the table and sloshing lemonade over the side of her glass. In an uncharacteristic move, she ignored the spill and instead began to pace. The glaring sunlight glinted off her glasses and made tiny flashing shapes onto the walls. Then all at once she stopped pacing. "Is that how she made us time travel?"

James rose slowly. "That's what I'm thinking."

"And it broke?" Mary's voice was barely a squeak. "When?"

"In 1955."

17

Run for Your Life

"No!" May's scream rose up from somewhere deep and couldn't be contained. She sprang out from behind the holly hedge and Row grasped at her friend's skirt. The men who had been working their way down the street shoving Judah Jackson between them and beating him when he fell their way paused.

Finigan leaped in front of May protectively. Then Row was on her feet, trying to hold back both her friend and her dog.

"Well, well," one of the filthiest of the soldiers stumbled their way. "What do we have here?"

"Let them be!" wheezed Judah with what sounded like his last breath. For speaking, he got a punch in the stomach.

"Our dog escaped the barn," Row said. "We came to bring him back home." Her voice shook.

"He attacks the neighbors' chickens," May added. She was trying to buy time, assess how they could possibly help Judah escape. Not only did she fear for his life, but she didn't know how the rest of them would fare without his help getting into Illinois via the raging Mississippi River.

"Git that mutt and git out of here. This is none of yer concern!" snarled one of the men, snorting and then spitting. May thought what an animal he was, but then realized that he was nothing like Finigan. She wanted to scream a threat at the men, or cause a distraction, but her mind raced senselessly, wildly, and she struggled in vain against her powerlessness.

Once again, Judah was tossed to another man in their loose and staggering circle, and as if reading May's and Row's desperation, Finigan launched himself on the man who was about to kick Judah.

"Fin!" screamed Row, but it was too late. He was in a tangle of wild men, who were swearing, cursing, and striking out. It was not enough of a distraction to get Judah, who barely had the energy to stand, away. Now May was holding Row back and when the shot rang out, they both froze. May couldn't breathe at all, but a sob escaped Row.

Finigan fell to the ground in a heap, and Judah echoed the movement, falling to his knees. At first, May and Row couldn't tell who, if anyone, had been shot; but then a red pool began to form under Fin's body. Judah's head hung, not so much in distress over the dog, but over his own pain and weariness—his own treatment as less than a dog.

As May and Row stood in a daze, the soldiers themselves paused for a brief moment, taking in what had just happened, and Judah raised his chin just enough to meet the girls' eyes from across the dimly lit street. "Go. Now. Go home. This is your fault. Go." And then he followed Finigan down, collapsing a few yards away from the dog.

May felt stabbed in the heart! Her fault. Hers.

"No," whimpered Row, all other words meaningless, not sure even what her "no" signified. No to all of it; to where they were, to Finigan dying in the street, to Judah being assaulted and slowly murdered, to her friend Emily somewhere waiting for them. To her brothers and mother being gone for good. To war. To hate. To hopelessness.

"Let's go, Row," May whispered. "Let's go."

Row remained frozen, dazed.

"Let's go!" May screamed, finally rousing her friend.

The soldier with the gun raised it toward the girls for sport, not to shoot, but to see them frightened. It worked. Seeing the gun pointed at them rallied May and Row and they bolted, running away from the soldiers and the bloody scene.

Moments later, the girls collapsed by the side of a house, not sure where they were or how far they'd run. May hadn't realized she'd been sobbing. Row grasped her, squeezing her, as much to warm both of them as to try to console May. "It's not your fault, Marion," she said into May's cold hair.

"It is," insisted May. "And we can't go back now. We've got to find Em and the others and get them across the river. They'll need us now more than ever." She hiccuped and tried to catch her breath, but the tears still came. "I'm —I'm sorry about Fin. He was a good dog."

Row took a deep, rattling breath. She couldn't think about Fin right now. Or else she'd think about . . . . "He was trying to protect us. So let's do what we can to make his life worth it. We don't have the luxury of feeling sorry right now."

Marion took a shaky breath, trying to steady herself. But it took several minutes for the wracking, involuntary sobs to subside. "I wish we'd wake up," she moaned.

"I know. I know," sighed Row.

The worst day of Row's life had been when her dad picked her up at school in the middle of the day last January. He had come and stood at her classroom door, with the principal by his side. Row had seen him walk up, but pretended she didn't, going back to her composition for what she was sure was the last moment in her life of ignorant bliss—if you could call it that—and normality. She'd had nothing left to lose; her brothers were already gone. There had been no reason for her father to be standing expectantly waiting on her and looking so stricken, unless it was something terrible about Row's mother.

Tommy Twigler had given her a look of pity on her way out the door. She had thought, "What do you know, anyway, you old orphan?" at the knowing, syrupy-sweet, sympathetic expression on his face. But she'd instantly regretted it. Not just because of Twig, but because she knew another orphan that she loved: Emily.

These had been the nonsensical thoughts that batted around in her brain on the way home in her dad's red 1942 Studebaker Champ. When she thought back now—which she rarely did—she couldn't remember if anyone had ever actually explicitly told her that her mom had died. Her grandparents had been at the house, tear-stained but trying to appear stoic. They'd taken her across town for her to stay a few days with them, and Row had regretted it every day since. That had been when their neighbor Gladys had swooped in to help her dad with funeral arrangements. Gladys not long after became Row's stepmother.

But Row had been in too much of a fog to think clearly, to insist on staying to help her dad. It hadn't been the actual loss of her mother that had shaken her, although that was dreadful in itself. It had been the idea that something so horrible could happen. Row had decided that previous June, with the last officer visit telling them *of her nineteen-year-old brother Kell's decease in the Battle of the Philippine Sea, that there would be no more tragedy in her or her family's life. It was a decision she'd intended to stick to. So she had been stunned that it hadn't been up to her. Tragedy had struck again and she had been powerless to prevent it.*

But not tonight. Rowena still had a chance tonight to make it right. Maybe she couldn't bring her brothers, her mother . . . or her dog . . . back, but she could help Marion and she could help Emily. And she could help Gin, Noah, and Eliza. She touched the locket around her neck, willing it to provide strength she didn't have.

"Are you ready?" Row asked May. "You have to help find the church."

May nodded. Taking a deep breath, they steadied each other and started out again, heading down a parallel street so they wouldn't go near the scene of the horrific incident they had just witnessed. They picked up the pace and began running, May feeling more alert and spotting the steeple much sooner than she had anticipated. She wondered briefly why Judah had been going the opposite direction until she realized that he had been leading the soldiers away from the church. She and Row had been coming from the wrong direction and he'd never expected the girls to be anywhere near where he'd ended up. Her throat tightened once more, but seeing the steeple helped her steel her resolve.

"That's it," she whispered to Row. They took the long way around the block to come to the back of the church. They urged open the cellar doors, which were obscured by hedges from the street and the outbuildings adjacent to the chapel. Climbing down the steep stone steps slick with icy moisture, May was tempted to weep again, she was so relieved to be off the street. When they got to the bottom, they

pushed into the darkness, wondering if they were alone after all, needing to wait for the others.

And then Row tripped on something and there was a soft grunt.

"Em?"

"Row? May?"

Gin struck a match and lit a gas lamp and at once the group clung together in a hug.

Eliza, holding a well-swaddled, sleeping Noah, touched May's arm. She said simply, "Judah gone."

"I—I know. We saw him."

"You seen him?" Gin asked in hushed surprise. They continued to keep their voices low.

May nodded, but couldn't speak for a moment. And then started to explain, "He was captured—"

"He led the soldiers away from us and away from the church. He the bravest man I ever did know," Eliza said fervently.

"I'm sorry about Judah," May rushed to say. "He told me it was my fault. I know he's right and I'm sorry."

"He say that?" Eliza said.

When May nodded with a pained expression, Gin offered, "He say that to save yo life. So you don' stay around tryin' ta help him when you should be comin' ta fine us."

"Really?" May whispered.

"He the bravest man I ever did know," Eliza echoed her earlier statement.

"Let us pray," Gin put in and followed with a heartfelt prayer. They then moved to the other side of the cellar where there was an opening in the stone wall, about two feet in diameter. May had been grasping Row's and Em's hands and now she saw the tunnel and felt she might pass out as she even thought about being enclosed in the small space.

"It only 'bout eight feet long," Eliza assured May, seeing the look on her face. How could May give it another second's concern after what Eliza had been through her whole life and just now, losing Judah? May nodded bravely and volunteered to go first.

❖　❖　❖

Emily had been pleasantly surprised by Eliza's grace under pressure. Em had expected Gin to be their fearless leader, but Eliza had been the one to step up. When on their way to the church to meet Row and May, Noah had been fussy, and a band of soldiers, out way past curfew, had heard the crying. Eliza had looked sharply at Judah and said simply, "Go." Without hesitating, he'd run out toward the soldiers, pretending to be searching for an escaped, bleating goat.

On the move again, without looking back, Eliza had silently urged Em and Gin away from the church to circle around and come back to it from another direction. They had waited in the dark for what felt like an infinite night, but Judah had never come. At last, May and Row had arrived. Now, trudging through the dank, chilly caves on their way to their next "station" or safe house, Em thought sadly of Judah and wondered how Eliza seemed to hold her head high and keep going so easily.

Each step felt like an eternity, and yet the night was slipping away too fast. They needed to cross the river into Illinois well before daybreak with enough time to get to Alton. They arrived at the first station, where very few words were exchanged, but the elderly married couple gave them water and biscuits and a wool blanket to share between them.

The white woman said, "Thought there was one more?"

To which Gin replied simply, "We lost one. But he led some bush-whackers away from us." The conductor gave a curt nod, but offered a sympathetic look at Gin; then, seeing Eliza with the baby, he gave Eliza a sad expression, too, for good measure.

Soon, with directions the rest of the way to the river, the group was back on the way toward freedom, heading through a series of caves, back up onto the street through alleyways, and back down through underground tunnels again.

Em hobbled in the birthday shoes that she had stolen back from Willimina as though her feet were being stabbed through with needles and knives. But not once did she slow down, ask to rest, or make any gesture toward inspecting the damage. Em was thinking of Willimina with every step. And Crawford. And Judah. But most of all, she thought of Noah. She wanted him to have no memory of having been enslaved.

They could tell they were getting close to the Mississippi because of the smells of its wet mud and the smoke from the riverboats' black fumes. And then, suddenly, they were upon it, the huge, twisting, silver snake that slithered between them and freedom. Twenty precarious steps winding downward would bring them to a skiff, tucked in leafless shrubs and tied to a birch tree. Before they descended, feeling an unbearable mix of relief, anxiety, joy, and exhaustion, they paused for a breath.

May reached for her friend Row's hand, but there was no one there. She turned to look behind her just as Em gasped, "Fin?"

Row was running away from the river, dropping to her knees. She threw herself gently on a bloody, war-torn-looking dog. Em was shocked; the creature looked exactly like Row's dog from 1945!

Gin took a few steps to kneel next to Row and inspect the dog. "Shot clean through," she concluded, shaking her head.

"He saved us from the soldiers who caught Judah," Row whispered. "Will he make it?"

Gin shook her head again, but not to say no. To express her wonder. "Came this far," she said. She got up and took the blanket that was around Eliza's shoulders and put it around the dog. Eliza didn't protest. Em and May wrapped the dog in the blanket and tied a piece of rope around it to form a kind of large tourniquet around Fin's middle.

"We best keep movin'." Gin went back to the edge of the steep slope to the river and took the first few steps down.

"We have to leave him, Row," Em whispered to her friend. Row nodded in agreement and gave Fin one last hug. He licked her face and even in the dim moonlight, Em saw the pure love in Row's eyes. Em and May helped Row up and made their way toward the ledge and then down the wide, uneven stone slabs that formed stairs to the river's edge.

As they dragged the vessel away from the shrubs and toward the lapping shoreline, Em wondered if they should scramble back up the bank and try to bring Finigan with them across the river. The thought of losing one more, even if it was a dog, was too much to consider.

Her impractical scheme was washed away with the strong currents of the Mississippi, however, because the moment they pushed away from the shore, they were in a battle to keep from drowning.

18

Salvation of a Single Soul

The currents were unrelenting. Four of them rowed at a time while one held the baby, and then they rotated —when one was convinced her arms would fail from exhaustion from paddling, she would take baby Noah and trade him for the oar. They kept their gaze fixed on the Illinois side, not once turning to look behind them. Em was terrified they would capsize the boat and lose Noah. She forced herself to think dry, Illinois-side, shore-like thoughts.

After what felt like weeks but was probably more like an hour and a half, they had crossed what was one of the narrowest passages of the river (but which was still triple the width of any other typical waterway). Gin and Emily staggered out of the boat and heaved it onto the rocks of Illinois. The boat teetered, its passengers losing their balance and then gripping the sides and straightening it by sheer will. With Emily's arms and torso screaming in pain from the exertion of rowing, she no longer thought about the discomfort in her feet and legs.

She thought nonsensically of her toe shoes and longed to put them on for a performance in an auditorium where she would be safe and sound. She knew she was getting delirious when she imagined both of her grandparents, her dead parents, and Eliza, Gin, Noah, and Judah sitting in the front row to see her performance. Eras, generations, and lifetimes blended into one moment. She wanted to weep for their need to take this journey in the first place, and she wanted to laugh with relief that they'd made it this far.

Thanks to the currents, they had landed further south than they had anticipated and would have to make up the distance north toward Alton on foot. Outside of Alton, a wagon would meet them and take them to the next station, where they would eat and rest until nightfall.

As they struggled up the embankment, Gin instructed them, "Don' look back. Never look back."

As much as Row, Em, and May wanted to gaze across the river to mark the distance they'd come—and Row to see if she could catch a glimpse of Finigan—they obeyed Gin, keeping their eyes ahead and their bodies moving forward, even as they crested the bank of the Mississippi and turned northward.

The edges of the sky hinted at the approaching dawn and the moon had crossed the sky. Emily thought how the periwinkle ring of pale light could have signified twilight just as easily as dawn. She had never known being a refugee could be so disorienting, or that finding out her true heritage could tear the foundation right out from under her.

❖   ❖   ❖

Judy woke before dawn even though she'd gone to sleep only two hours before. She was too excited to sleep. Today was the day Diane Dunkelman would be held accountable for her terrible misdeeds and Maxine would be justified and presented with the surprise Judy and her friends had worked on most of the night. Judy was thrilled that she now knew enough about the computer that she could email James her final project. She wondered how Mary would fare with her project without any computer skills.

Unrolling her hair, she evaluated herself in the mirror. What if today she didn't wear pigtails? What if she just wore it in messy half curls like so many of the girls around school? This morning she felt bold enough to try it, hoping she'd look like a modern-day Doris Day, and pulled a light yellow spring dress over her head. She took extra care getting ready and was still in the kitchen before her mom.

Judy had taught herself how to use the coffee maker that her mom had bought (but never used) to save money on drive-thru lattes. As Judy watched the rivulet of hot, bitter liquid drizzle into the carafe, Bitsy appeared.

Surprised, she noted, "You're up early."

"A big day," Judy enthused.

"Me, too. I need coffee. Roger has me doing the presentation for what could be our number two client—if they sign with us. I need coffee," she repeated, reaching past Judy for the pot and then over Judy's head to get a mug from the cabinet, even though Judy had two cups waiting on the counter.

Judy hoped her mom would ask why it was such a big day for her daughter, but the moment never came. Bitsy prattled on about her presentation and Roger Streeter. The longer she talked, the more disheartened Judy felt. In 1955, Bitsy would have asked Judy about her day at school, wished her well for her coming day, and known about Judy's most recent dreams and adventures, hopes, and fears. Judy didn't know if the future or Roger Streeter was to blame. But at the moment, both were leaving a more bitter taste in her mouth than the black coffee.

"Aren't you using any sweetener or milk?" Bitsy paused from her monologue long enough to ask Judy.

Oh, swell. That *she notices.* "I'm cutting back on fattening calories," Judy said as her lunch with Bob, Diane, Carla, and the rest of the popular kids came rushing to mind.

Bitsy didn't comment, but gulped down the rest of her morning fuel and kissed the top of Judy's head absently. For a brief moment, Judy felt like it was 1955 again and wanted to gush to her mom about her acting job with Diane Dunkelman, and how she and her friends were rallying to try to help Maxine. But as quickly as it came, the moment was gone, and Bitsy was off to get ready for her day while Judy went to wait for her ride.

She watched for the Jenkins' car from the porch, the heat of the day already radiating from every surface. When the car appeared, she felt nostalgic for the pale green Buick of 1955. She dashed to the shiny dark silver sedan, opened the back door, and popped in next to Bev, calling out a perky, "Hiya!"

Her mood mellowed when she saw Gary behind the wheel instead of Bob. Reading her expression, Bev muttered, "Bob's out."

"Oh." Judy slumped.

"But I'm in," Gary said cheerily. "Good morning."

Gary, Bev, and Judy had agreed to meet James at the copy shop to help with any last-minute details and make 200 copies of volume 1 of *The Visible Truth*. Judy set aside her disappoint-ment over Bob's not being there to focus on what this project would mean to her friend, Maxine, and her excitement level rose again.

"What did you decide to do for your project, Bev?"

"I did a play-by-play of Maxine winning the game," Bev said, rolling her eyes. "Only for Maxine would I do something like this when I'm not even being graded on it. I hope my idea's not too dumb."

"It's clever," encouraged Gary. "Do you mind if I put on some tunes?" He turned up the music in the car and Judy and Bev both wrinkled their noses. Bev shook her head, thinking, *If Mom and Pops thought* Elvis *was bad, they should hear this.*

They arrived at the copy store to find James and Mary already waiting for them. Greetings went around the group and Mary gave Judy an extra long hug. "I'm glad you're not *really* friends with Diane Dunkelman," she whispered into Judy's ear.

Judy smiled, but something tugged at her heart. She was secretly starting to hope she could be friends with Diane *and* the Fifties Chix. But then Mary said, "Your hair looks boss, Judy," in all sincerity, and Judy remembered: Diane never would have complimented Judy like that.

❖   ❖   ❖

Judy held the first *Visible Truth*, hot off the copier. She breathed in the smell of warm paper and toner. It was more magical than a mimeograph: stacks and pages of words and images in an instant.

"Isn't that the best smell?" James said.

Judy flipped through the small volume eagerly, seeing written pieces and familiar names pass with each page. She stopped at a beautiful depiction of a cluster of radiant purple-blue flowers that looked like they were lit from inside. "Wow," she breathed.

"That's Ann's," Gary said. "She painted it all night. The original's not even dry yet. Before we picked you up, I offered to go to her house and take a picture of it."

Bev smirked. "Gee, how generous—" She stopped as Gary elbowed his sister to shut her up.

"Oh, Mary. Here's yours. You wrote a poem?" Judy said, beginning to read it.

Mary blushed and kept her eyes averted from Ann and James. She reached out and shut the paper. "We'll have lots of time to read them all later." She seemed to be turning redder.

"This was such a nice thing to do for Maxine," Judy said with a faraway dreamy look.

"It's not just for the salvation of a single soul—Maxine's; it's for all of us. Especially the kids at school who just don't get it," Gary said.

"Like Diane Dunkelman," snorted Bev.

Gary added, "And our brother Bob."

Judy's face fell. Maybe this wasn't going to be as fun as she thought.

19

Willing Suspension of Disbelief

Maxine sat at the desk in her room. Today she was suspended from school. But she still got up at the usual time and made all the usual preparations. She even read her daily scripture, choosing to read the twenty-third Psalm for comfort. In turning to the worn page in her Bible, she glanced at Psalm 27: *Though an host should encamp against me, my heart shall not fear: though war should rise against me, in this will I be confident.* Her heart swelled with relief that despite what was going on around her, on the inside she could be confident in the truth of who she was.

After a simple breakfast of dry toast, the house was quiet— her parents at work and her sister, Melba, starting her summer job—and Maxine wondered what to do with a whole day "off" from school. The hours stretched out before her, ending at a tiny dot in the evening that she couldn't see from where she sat. She held her grandmother's quill in her hand and gazed at it. She had an imaginary conversation with the feather-tipped pen that went something like this: *"It's not your fault; you were just doing your job."*

"So were you," the quill answered.

While she was being suspended by the school for a crime—threatening violence—she hadn't committed, maybe Maxine was being suspended by the universe for being indulgent in writing an essay that was bound to be misunderstood.

The sound of the doorbell made her start and snapped Maxine out of her musings. She wondered who could be coming by when it was still so early in the morning. As she crossed the small living room, she could see through the gauzy curtains what looked like a small crowd gathered on the front lawn. Her heart took off at a sprint, wondering if she should pretend that no one was home. She peered through the peephole and was surprised to see Judy, Bev, Mary, and Ann congregated on the stoop. She swung the door open to see that behind the girls, in the yard, were Conrad, Gary, James, and a few of their friends.

"We're going to miss you at school today and we thought you might like to take a break from all that writing you do and do some reading for once," smiled Judy. She held out a booklet to Maxine. It looked just like underground paper Maxine had written for, but this one had a bright green cover and read *The Visible Truth*. The girls converged on Maxine for a hug.

"What is this?" Maxine asked and started to flip through it. Immediately she saw an essay titled, *My Sister, The Strong One; by Melba Marshall*. Maxine's heart skipped a beat.

Judy pointed and stated the obvious. "Your sister wrote that one."

"We all contributed," Mary added.

"Except for B—" Judy started, but she stopped herself and tried a new tack: "I'm sorry for what I said to you at my house. I've been trying to get close to Diane because I knew she was behind that page on the Internet, and I was right. I'm telling Principal Jones today."

"Hey, Maxine. Great essay," Gary called from the lawn. To everyone else, he encouraged, "We gotta get going. I have a test in AP English this morning."

Everyone said their reluctant goodbyes and Ann fit in another embrace, whispering, "Friends forever."

Maxine hated to see them go, but was grateful for the return to solitude so that she could cry in private.

Mary's heart was in her throat. She sat in the office, in one of those ugly molded plastic chairs against the wall. She had just been sent to the office the week before for being smart with a substitute teacher, so when she was called out of third period this time, she wondered at her crime. She assumed she must be in trouble for her part in the publishing of *The Visible Truth*, but even Mrs. F and Maxine's parents had written something for it, so she couldn't imagine that her involvement with that would warrant a visit to the school counselor, Mrs. Snyder, again.

Her day had started off so well. James had picked her up before her mother, Nana, or the kids were awake and brought her to the all-night copy place. She was thrilled to get a peek into James's world; his eyes glittered and his cheeks were flushed with excitement as they worked on the project for Maxine. He organized scraps of paper and worked on his laptop computer, adjusting, reorganizing, and occasionally printing things out and readjusting on his computer. Watching him, Mary got a glimpse of James's future—his *real* future, as a young man, making a difference helping people as a journalist. She'd had a hunch of how bright and motivated he was, but to see him in action made her realize that what had threatened her so much before—his appreciation of her friends—was one of the many things she actually had come to adore about him.

When the student aide had come in to Mary's home sciences class and handed a slip of paper to Mrs. Doss, who had called out Mary's name, Mary had immediately flushed. Her wonderful memories—of James and all her friends and presenting *The Visible Truth* to Maxine right before school started—had flown right out of her mind as the students in the class eyed Mary critically. She collected her books and nervously left class with sweaty palms and a heart pounding double time.

After the bell rang to start fourth period and many students had come and gone from the office, the secretary at last told Mary she could go see Mrs. Snyder. Mary nearly knocked the row of chairs over as she sprang to her feet and tripped her way toward Mrs. Snyder's door.

Mrs. Snyder was on the phone, but waved Mary in. Mary sat precariously on the edge of her seat while Mrs. Snyder finished her call. After assuring a concerned parent that only his son's best SAT scores would be sent to college admissions, Mrs. Snyder hung up and shuffled papers on her desk. Absentmindedly, she greeted Mary.

"Aha!" she said at last, grabbing a sheet of paper and handing it to Mary.

Mary looked at the paper, titled "M. Fairview—Retirement Celebration."

"What's this?" Mary asked.

"You were in my office recently and you said Mrs. Fairview was your favorite teacher."

Mary waited for Mrs. Snyder to continue, but the counselor seemed to have already moved to the next order of business, stacking folders and clicking on her computer keyboard.

"She is," Mary said, urging Mrs. Snyder on.

"Oh. Right. Sorry. Well, as you know, she's retiring this year. We're doing a school-wide assembly and I'm in charge of it. I'm swamped, as you can see, and I thought of you." Mrs. Snyder paused long enough to look at Mary, who still was waiting for more information. "I thought of you and wondered if you'd like to organize a theme or something for the assembly. A look back at her career and life, like—"

"'This is Your Life'!" Mary said eagerly.

Mrs. Snyder laughed, surprised that Mary knew what she had been about to say. Not many kids these days knew about that old show. "Exactly."

"I'd love to!" Mary was flushed again, but this time with excitement. "Thank you for asking me. It's an honor, truly."

Mrs. Snyder laughed again. "OK," she said slowly. Another thing about kids these days, at least the ones visiting her office: not too jazzed about extra projects. Except for Mary. "Unfortunately, we only have a week."

"That's fine."

"Oh. And you might find these helpful." Mrs. Snyder reached behind her desk to hand Mary a stack of books. "These are yearbooks from when Mrs. Fairview went to school here. Can you believe it? She went here all those years ago. Only then her name was—"

"Miss Boggs."

"Well, looks like I chose the right person! That's right; her name was Marion Boggs. So have fun looking through those and let's be in touch. Let me know your ideas, and the more you can come up with in terms of a plan, the better."

Mrs. Snyder passed Mary a card with Mrs. Snyder's email address and direct phone line on it. Mary barely looked at it, transfixed by the yearbooks stacked in her arms. She felt like she had struck gold. She and Mrs. Snyder both said distracted good-byes.

❖   ❖   ❖

"Marion!"

For a foggy, delayed moment, May was so disoriented, she couldn't even recognize the voices of her best friends, Em and Row. They crouched over her, eagerly calling to her and shaking her gently awake. She sat up suddenly, hungrily taking in her surroundings.

She gasped. Row's room. Pale blue, with pictures of the Nolan brothers and the modern decor of the 1940s. May's friends' eyes were wide with the same bewilderment and relief. May bolted to a sitting position. "What . . . ?"

"We don't know. Em just woke me up and we saw you . . . . All we know is we're here. Now." Row scrambled to her feet and her body's memory of the previous night's exertion slowed her immediately. She opened her bedroom door and was met by a black dog leaping onto her. They collapsed onto the floor together, Finigan

licking her frantically, tail wagging so hard it was about to come off. Row laughed and cried, holding Fin against her.

Shocked and exhausted, Em and May crawled over and joined them. After a few moments, they tried to catch their breath and get their bearings. May's right hand went to her left wrist, and when she felt nothing there, she studied the bare patch of skin where the gold watch should have been.

"The watch!" she breathed.

Missing also were Row's necklace and locket and Emily's shoes.

"Don't you remember?" Emily said. "The bounty hunters Dunkelman sent out caught up to us and threatened to shoot if we didn't go with them. You jumped in front of their guns and offered to pay for Gin, Eliza, Noah, and me with the watch."

Row nodded wildly. May wracked her brain with as much energy as she'd expended in paddling, but couldn't recall anything beyond the color of the night sky. "How did we get here, then?"

Row said, still stroking Fin as if her life depended on it, "The last thing I remember is a shot rang out and everything went dark. I thought I had died, but I woke up here with Em shaking me."

"That's all I remember, too," Emily said. "How do we know if Eliza, Gin, and Noah made it?" She was suddenly in a panic.

Row and May looked at each other. "Why, because you're here," May reasoned. "Noah is your grandfather."

"I suppose," Em agreed, but her shoulders slumped and her eyes welled with tears. She whispered, "We have to go back."

❖   ❖   ❖

Maxine closed the door behind her as tears of joy blurred her vision. As quickly as they fell, she swiped to clear them away so she could read *The Visible Truth*. Before she could even make her way to the living room and sit down, she began reading where the paper had randomly fallen open:

The Power of the Quill

Once there was a girl who wanted nothing more than the truth. Sometimes the truth felt like the air everybody breathes without a thought about it ever running out; but she felt it was running out for her and she was suffocating. Without knowing the truth about her past, she was sure she could not make her way into the future. But time is a funny thing. It marches on whether you are ready or not.

The Bible tells us the truth makes us free. It may make us free from lies, but it doesn't make us free from complications, free from responsibility or free from regret.

This girl was my friend. Those who loved her saw her as a beam of light; she radiated love. She was not a race or a color; she was not a size or a shape. She was the spark in my day. I couldn't wait to see her shining face when I woke up in the morning. I couldn't wait to see how she would make me laugh that day. She was a talented dancer. She moved with grace and vigor on stage and through her life. But still she felt something was missing. In short order, she got her wish: she did discover the truth.

I will never forgive myself for helping her find what she was looking for. I thought she was lost and needed to be found, but now she is lost to me. I thought I had sacrificed much to help her; but no, it was selfish because I did it all for me: to see her smile. To keep her in my life. And now, even now, all these years later, I know how she felt, missing something so essential. Because she is missing from my life.

This is what I've learned: in our search for truth, we cannot forget to love. One is not more important than the other. If sometimes we have to lay aside our quest for truth to love instead, it is not a failure and the journey has not ceased. Instead, we may just find a shortcut.

Your future is not determined by your past. It is determined by this moment, right now. Love, right here and right now, who you are and who your friends are. Then you will find truth. Then you will be free.

Marion G. Boggs Fairview

Mrs. F's words invigorated Maxine and she wondered what it all meant: who the girl was, and why Mrs. F had titled the essay "The Power of the Quill." Beyond those questions, the message was clear. It was what Mrs. F—back when she was Miss Boggs —had made the girls promise: to be friends forever. It wasn't that Miss Boggs had *requested* that they do it; she had made them *promise* to do it. That and nothing else.

Maxine realized with a start that she had been angry with her friends for not knowing her, not understanding—or trying to understand—her; but what had Maxine done to understand them? What had she done to demonstrate her faithfulness as a friend? Wiping her tears, Maxine's eye caught Mrs. F's words: *she radiated love. She was not a race or a color; she was not a size or a shape.* Maxine realized that it was time for all of them to stop seeing themselves as a race or color, size or shape, and start seeing themselves as *friends*.

20

Good as New

Rowena Nolan did not consider herself a nervous person. But she was grateful to be wearing gloves because the fabric soaked up the sweat of her palms. She had even taken pains to put on lipstick, which made her feel manipulative. Hadn't she known that Twig had had a crush on her in high school? Was she taking advantage? Well, she would do what she needed to make it right. To help Marion and maybe even bring back Emily.

Her hand shook as she turned the knob and pushed the door to the shop open. Bells hanging from the door clattered and made her heart skip a beat. Clocks lined the walls and filled every surface, all clicking, ticking, and tocking to their own beat. It was a cacophony of rhythm that in any other situation Row might have found amusing, but now found disconcerting.

She closed the door behind her and walked straight to the counter. The store was like a tunnel, only twelve feet wide, leading to a cluttered counter with a register that looked like it was from the Civil War. Row shook off her nerves at the thought.

"Hello?" she called out.

A man came out from a door behind the cash register, a preoccupied expression on his face. He was not expecting—or wanting—to be disturbed. Until he looked up to see who had just walked through his door.

"Tommy."

"Row?" Twig asked in wonder. He nearly threw down the silver antique watch he was polishing, but managed to keep his composure. While he tried not to lunge at her, she tried not to lunge back out the door to escape to her dad's one-year-old 1954 black Ford Crestline she'd parked out on the street. "I tried to call—"

"I know." Row straightened her hat. The pins were digging into her scalp. She'd rather be wearing a sun hat and working in the garden than primped up wearing a girdle and makeup. She had no tolerance for pleasantries, didn't want to talk about the weather or fabricate excuses for why she hadn't called after she'd gone on two dates with him. He'd been asking for years. When May had gotten engaged, Row had finally conceded to date Tommy Twigler. But she'd had an ulterior motive then and she had one now, and it wasn't about going steady with him. She cut to the chase. "I want the watch back."

Twig looked away, not willing to meet her eyes. He gingerly placed the watch he was holding on the counter, then picked it back up again for something to do. He cleared his throat. "It's busted, you said so yourself."

"You and I both know it's not broken, Twig. What did you do with it? I want it back." Row was barely a minute in to their conversation and she felt herself starting to panic. When Twig took a beat too long to answer, she rushed to say, "I brought something in trade."

This intrigued Twig. "What is it?"

She unfolded her left hand, which had been cramped into a tight fist. Taking a step forward, she held it out to him. Before she snatched her hand back, which she desperately wanted to do, Twig took the gold necklace and glittering heart-shaped pendant from her gloved palm. It caught the mid-summer sunlight coming in the window and sparkled so bright in Row's eye, she nearly teared up. It made even the dingy clock shop look special.

"It's beautiful, to be sure, but—"

Row couldn't take no for an answer. She hadn't taken the necklace off since her mother had given it to her for her twelfth birthday in 1942. For thirteen years, friends had asked what the locket meant and what it contained. For thirteen years, she'd kept the secret her mother had asked her to and never told a soul. Not even May or Em. For thirteen years, she'd felt the smooth gold locket brushing against her collarbone, not taking it off for even a moment, except for one. . . .

In an instant, standing with Twig, Row remembered the conversation her mother had had with her when all the cake had been eaten, the presents ripped open, and all the fun of her twelfth birthday left her stuffed, tired, and happy. Her brothers Orvan and Kell had scattered to be with their girlfriends before they were shipped out to fight in the war; Wally Jr. was already serving in the Army in North Africa and would be dead by Christmas, which of course none of them knew at the time. Em and May had gone back to their own homes. Row's father smoked a pipe on the porch in the early June setting sun. It occurred to Row then as she helped her mother clean up to ask whose picture was in the locket. She was certain that she knew the answer: her brothers. They were going to war and Row would be left an only child . . . temporarily, they prayed.

Row's mom had taken her by the hand, disregarding the dishes and the mess. "I want you to keep the locket always close to your heart. I want you to know how special you are. Your brothers are their own selves and they are going off to fight for this country; but you are a hero, too. You are in the locket, Rowena. It's a picture of you. Never lose sight of who you are, especially when things fall apart around you, but even when things are grand. No one needs to know who is in the locket. You know and that's what counts. Do you understand?"

Row had taken her free hand and placed it over the pretty charm. She'd nodded. It was the first and last time her typically easy-going mom had ever spoken to her quite like that. Row's family was fun, always willing to laugh; she knew her brothers had her back and she knew her parents loved her. But this had been a moment unlike any other and she'd known that it was as much a gift as the jewelry around her neck. She had never even opened it to see which picture of herself her mother had put in it until she had opened it to add a picture of her mom. She'd been moved to discover that the picture her mother had placed in the golden heart was Row as a baby being held by her mom. After that, Row felt like the inside of the locket should not ever be disturbed again; it was a sacred, tiny memorial that she shared with her mother.

Colliding with this memory was one in another time and place: the only situation where Row had taken the necklace off. Em, May, and she had been outside Alton, Illinois that cold morning in 1864. A bounty hunter had tracked them and Shelby Jackson's slaves down. The women and the baby had—impossibly—made it across the river, were breathing a sigh of relief. When the bounty hunter and his partner had approached the women, the weary refugees had hoped against hope the two men were farmers. But they hadn't been dressed like Lachlan and they'd had the sharp edge of men who were driven to find something—or someone.

While Gin and Eliza had remained stone cold and silent, Emily and May had pleaded with the men to let them go. They even offered to go in the place of the women and the baby. Row had been too stunned, too exhausted, and too scared to speak. But mostly, she had felt she'd already spent all her hope.

Then she'd felt a tug around her neck and realized that she had grasped her necklace and locket, pulling it off and saying, "We'll pay the bounty for them. I have this gold necklace and locket."

The sun had been rising rapidly and they were still at least a mile, they guessed, from their next station and certain safety.

Row's offer had gotten the men's attention, even though they'd tried to look uninterested.

"And I have this gold watch," May had piped up, pulling it off her wrist. Row's spirits had plunged. They would never get home without that watch. May had reminded her of it several times.

"And I have these . . . rare leather shoes." Emily held her shoes out to them.

The men had laughed, but stepped closer to take a look. The helper had lowered his gun and Row had felt herself take a breath for the first time in what felt like five minutes. "I think we'd rather get the reward," the tall man in the long black wool coat had said.

"Jackson's got no money," May had said steadily. "He's selling off his slaves. That's why we left, to be honest with you. They're going to the auction block. He's not going to pay you to get them back."

At this the men had taken pause. A spark of hope so hot it hurt had burned in Row's chest. Discussing it amongst themselves and inspecting the watch, the shoes, and the locket, the two men had finally agreed to take the trade.

The gun shots that had run out at that moment had made Row's heart stop. When she was next conscious, she was back in her room in 1945. Days later, she had found the locket in a box in her top dresser drawer.

It had taken Row months for the rest of the memory to take shape. The bounty hunters had fired guns to chase Row and her friends away when they'd seen Union soldiers headed their way. Since they were just barely out of Missouri, they would necessarily have been returned to Dunkelman and Jackson. Sprinting on pure adrenaline, they had arrived at their next safe station in Alton, foregoing meeting the wagon and driver as scheduled. After eating and slowing their heart rates enough to think clearly, Emily had reached under her clothes and presented Gin with a quill she said she'd stolen from Willimina Jackson's desk.

"We're free," Em had whispered to Gin. "You're free."

With that, they had all fallen happily asleep.

Now Twig held the locket up to inspect it like the bounty hunters had done.

Row explained how valuable the locket was, shamelessly playing on any affection Twig may have had or still had for her. She had tried to help May by getting the watch fixed, taking it to Twig because May had claimed it was broken. Row had worried that May would disregard the watch totally in an effort to start a new life with Reggie; Row wanted to present it to May as a wedding present, but it would be a few weeks overdue now. Row had realized too late that the watch might not have been broken just because she didn't know how to use it; May had just stopped wearing it—pretending, Row guessed, that it didn't exist. But with the five girls in May's class missing and Emily gone . . . . Well, giving up or pretending weren't options. May couldn't turn off her old life and just turn on a new one, like flipping a switch. Row wouldn't let her.

"I can't afford to buy it back. But I'm willing to give you my most precious possession in the whole world." Row's eyes were big and round.

"It really is broken," Twig said, still not looking her in the face. "I took it apart and have tried to fix it. Twice."

"You know what they say," Row said, trying be light and not shrill.

"What's that?"

"Third time's a charm."

"Is that what you'd say if I asked you on another date, Rowena?" Twig's confidence waned. He didn't look like the arrogant jock, a role he had played so easily in school and as a drafted pro football player; he actually blushed when he said it.

It made Row feel awful. She wasn't interested in Twig. She needed that watch back. But she couldn't lie. "Can you please just get the watch back to me in one piece?"

The door rattled and Rowena jumped.

Reginald Fairview, Row's best friend's husband, pushed through the entrance of Twig's dad's shop.

"Well, hello there, Row," Reggie said, as if he weren't the least bit surprised to find her there.

"Reggie," Row said simply. She got her bearings and asked what brought him in.

"Looking for a gift for Marion, of course." He and Twig greeted each other like old friends. Something didn't feel right. Row couldn't decide if she wanted to get out as soon as possible or linger to figure out what was going on.

"Maybe we can talk about this over dinner, Row?" Twig asked.

Row stood straighter. "I'm not going out with you, Tommy. I just want my—the—watch back."

The tunnel of a room was stifling and Row needed fresh air. But she vowed she wouldn't leave without that watch.

Reggie spoke up. "What watch is that? Let's see it, Twig."

Row could have sworn that Reggie and Twig smirked at each other before Twig ducked into the back room.

"How was the honeymoon?" Row asked, making conversation. Of course, she'd already talked to May about it. It was wonderful, May had gushed.

Reggie echoed his bride's sentiments. "Sadly," he added, "There's been a bit of a change in my business and I'll be traveling quite a bit. Not how you'd want to start a marriage; but I bought her a parrot for companionship. He even talks! May calls him Ike."

Row nodded. She'd heard Ike over the telephone but hadn't met him in person yet. She hadn't been too eager to, frankly. A talking bird! It made her miss good old Finigan.

A moment later, Twig returned with the familiar, freshly cleaned gold watch displayed on a piece of burgundy felt. Once again, Row restrained herself, this time from grabbing the watch. She felt as though she was seeing a dear friend after a long separation.

"It doesn't look broken," she said.

"Why, that's Marion's watch," Reggie said. His surprise didn't sound genuine.

"I brought it in to get it fixed," Row rushed to say.

"It looks good as new. Why can't she have it, Twig?"

Twig's mouth popped open. His surprise did look genuine. "She —she said she couldn't pay for it."

"I'm happy to pay for it. You're giving it back to May, right, Rowena? How much, Twig?"

Twig appeared to be at a loss for words.

Reggie said, "Twig is starting a new business and I'm going to be an investor. That's why I came in, Tommy; to tell you the good news. And now Marion's getting her watch back, too. What a grand day."

"It is, Mr. Fairview. Thank you," Twig smiled broadly and pulled out Row's hand. In it, he put her locket and the gold watch.

He never asked Row out on a date again, and sometimes Row wondered if he had asked one more time if she'd have said yes, she was so happy to have her locket back.

It had taken many years for Row to mention the strange scene in the clock shop to May. She hadn't understood it and felt like something was going on between Twig and Reggie. She hadn't realized they'd even known each other. For such a big city, St. Louis could seem like a small town. So Reggie and Tommy could very well have known each other, but that didn't account for the strange feeling she'd had in her gut. She didn't want to accuse Reggie of anything. And most of all, she could see how much he loved her friend and she convinced herself that was the only thing that mattered.

It wouldn't be until those girls showed up on her doorstep fifty-five years later that Rowena would tell Marion what she'd seen.

Epilogue

Emily didn't care any more about becoming a dancer. She no longer cared about moving to New York. And for once in her life, she didn't feel like she was running away from something. At last, she was running toward something.

She had a sister.

Viola Jackson had been in the car crash with Emily's parents and survived. The letter Emily held in her hand from her sister's foster parents confirmed it. Em wasn't supposed to have found the letter. Her grandmother insisted that she was going to tell Em on her twenty-first birthday. After an emotional scene wherein Emily demanded facts and details that had been denied her all her life, Grandma Parks all but confessed that she and Grandpa Parks had only been able to take one of the girls and had chosen the one who looked most white. Em didn't even feel angry. She just felt great pity. Sadness that her grandparents were so lacking in love that they could give away their own grandchild because of the color of her skin. No matter how much Grandma Parks tried to convince Em that they had wanted the best for Viola, Em knew they had really wanted the easy way out for themselves. Emily had considered briefly, but quickly rejected, the idea of telling her grandparents about her and Viola's true ancestry as descendants of a slave and slave owner. It made her sick to think how alone she had felt her whole life when she'd had a sister all along.

Emily had wanted the truth about her family and the truth just kept coming. But the more she knew, the less she knew herself. She didn't sleep nights, stopped going to dance lessons. She was late for school. She gave up laughter as if it was a luxury she couldn't afford. She didn't even notice when Tommy Twigler or Peter Jenkins tried to get her attention with their shenanigans.

Her friends worried. Row and May knew that Emily had been rattled by learning her true heritage as the grandchild of a slave and slave master and by their harrowing experience in 1860s St. Louis. But that was only part of it. She hadn't told them about Viola (whom she suspected was named for Violet, the slave girl who hadn't been able to go with Judah, Eliza, and baby Noah. She wondered what had happened to Violet and put finding out on her list of to-dos).

Emily left two days after Christmas to search for her sister. She didn't know how to begin looking and the thought had occurred to her that actually her friends could probably help her. But until she knew who she was, she couldn't be a friend to them. It wasn't that they were strangers to her, it was that she had become a stranger. She promised herself she would write a letter to Row and May as soon as she was far enough away that they wouldn't try to keep her from going. And so, quietly, in the darkness that inhabits all space before dawn, not unlike another escape she'd made in the not-so-distant past, she slipped out of her house without telling a soul.

When her grandparents woke up, they would find nothing but her favorite pair of now badly worn shoes lying next to her empty bed.

Glossary

Battle of the Philippine Sea: the largest aircraft carrier battle in history, fought between the US and Japan in World War II from June 19-20, 1944. It was a decisive battle off the Mariana Islands that the US won.

Camp Jackson: a Confederate arsenal in a park-like setting in St. Louis, Missouri (now near St. Louis University) where Union soldiers raided in May 1861. The details of the raid and the bloody events following it are outlined in chapter 7 of this book and are mostly accurate. Missouri had some of the bloodiest battles in the Civil War and the Camp Jackson Incident polarized and divided the citizens of Missouri.

Chump: a blockhead or a jerk; someone who's mad or eccentric

Civil War: a war fought essentially over slavery and waged on American soil from 1861-1865 between the Southern, or Confederate, states and the Northern, or Union, states. The Confederate states were: South Carolina, Mississippi, Florida, Alabama, Georgia, Louisiana, Texas, Virginia, Arkansas, Tennessee, and North Carolina. (Missouri and Kentucky were represented by partisan factions from those states, but were officially considered Union states.) Union states were: California, Connecticut, Illinois, Indiana, Iowa, Kansas, Maine, Massachusetts, Michigan, Minnesota, Nevada, New Hampshire, New Jersey, New York, Ohio, Oregon, Pennsylvania, Rhode Island, Vermont, and Wisconsin. Maryland and Delaware were "border states." Much of the Southern states' economy was dependent on slavery, and the South demanded states' right to govern themselves (i.e., have slaves) instead of being told by the federal government what to do. The war nearly split America into two countries; but since the Union ultimately won the war, the United States of America is one country and slavery is illegal.

Colored or **Negro:** terms used historically in reference to African Americans' skin tone ("colored" used for any skin tone darker than "white"), but also sometimes in a derogatory and disparaging way. In present day, the terms are certainly not appropriate because of the way many African Americans were derided and mistreated in association with the words.

Dollar: Before the Civil War, private banks issued hundreds of kinds of currency, but the US Treasury was authorized by Congress to issue official-looking bank notes to finance the war.

Emancipation Proclamation (also see **Civil War**, above): In September of 1862, President Lincoln "invited" the rebellious Southern states to rejoin the Union (the "United States" in the North); if they didn't, he said he would emancipate all slaves in the Confederate (Southern) states. None of the Confederate states took him up on the offer to return to Union control and so on January 1, 1863, President Lincoln issued the Emancipation Proclamation, freeing slaves. There was a catch to the proclamation, however: it only applied to the Confederate states. In border states such as Missouri, Kentucky, Maryland, and Delaware, slavery was still legal. Slavery didn't become illegal for all states until the ratification of the Thirteenth Amendment of the US Constitution in 1865.

Great Depression: a period in world history of severe economic depression that started with the stock market crash on what is known as "Black Tuesday," October 29, 1929 and lasting into World War II. A quarter of the US population was unemployed and farmers as well as industrialists were hit hard. Everyone learned to economize, making the most out of very little. Franklin D. Roosevelt was elected as President in 1933 and instituted many federal programs (called the New Deal) that created jobs and public works projects that helped America start to pull out of the financial crisis. Social Security came out of this era.

Kartoffelpuffer (German Potato Pancake) recipe: the Boggs household refrained from eating any German food during World War II, maybe because they were embarrassed to have a German background. This was one of May's favorite dishes and she was glad her mother started making it again when the war was over! Potato pancakes can be served with applesauce, sour cream, cheese, ketchup or even cinnamon and sugar.

Ingredients:
5 pounds of potatoes (3-4 medium sized potatoes make a pound)
2 large sweet onions
½ cup self-rising flour
2 large eggs
Salt and pepper to taste
Grate potatoes and onions together. Pour off excess juice, mix in eggs then add enough flour to thicken. Salt and pepper to taste. In large iron skillet, heat cooking oil; drop mixture into hot oil (about 2 inch pancakes). Brown to crisp on both sides. Serve hot.

Mad: crazy. Today we use "mad" mostly as a synonym for "angry," but in years past it more often meant "crazy."

Mudsill: a low-life; this word is a term for the lowest part of a structure that sits on or touches the ground. In 1858, it was used in a political speech in reference to disreputable people and became a slang term.

Mule: the offspring of a male donkey (a jack) and a female horse (a mare). Mules are intelligent, hard-working, and sure-footed animals that can endure harsher conditions than horses can and so are—and were—popular work animals on farms. Missouri was famous for the quality of mules it bred during the Civil War, and many farmers made a living breeding and selling mules.

Plantation: a working farm where the labor is made up of twenty slaves or more

Rations: tickets that were issued during World War II to families, allowing them to purchase only limited amounts of gasoline for their cars, food, and other supplies. The United States rallied in many ways that affected everyday life to support the war effort. Many materials and resources, like rubber, sugar, and metal, went toward the war effort.

Rin Tin Tin: a film, radio, and TV star who starred in 23 Hollywood movies and happens to be a dog! Rin Tin Tin was a German shepherd puppy first found on a battlefield in what is now France in World War I. An American soldier named Lee Duncan rescued him and brought him back to America when the war was over. Rin Tin Tin has a star on the Hollywood Walk of Fame and was given the keys to New York City by the Mayor of New York.

VE Day: "Victory in Europe Day," May 8, 1945; a day of great celebration in the United States, when Nazi Germany surrendered, ending World War II in Europe

VJ Day: "Victory over Japan Day" (August 14, 1945), when Japan surrendered, ending World War II

Wallis Simpson: an American socialite woman who in 1937 became Duchess of Windsor by marrying King Edward VIII. However, because she had two living ex-husbands, it caused a controversy and a political crisis in England and so Edward abdicated—gave up—the throne to be her husband. He became Prince Edward, Duke of Windsor, and his brother became King George VI. Though the story seems romantic on paper, the Duchess and Duke of Windsor continued to be a controversial couple and were suspected of being Nazi sympathizers during World War II.

BE KEPT IN ORBIT, HEP CATS!

1950 1960 1970 1980 *Fifties Chix* 1990 2000 2010 2020

Look for these other titles in the Fifties Chix series:

Book 1: Travel to Tomorrow
Book 2: Keeping Secrets
Book 4: Broken Record
Book 5: Till the End of Time

Check out **www.FiftiesChix.com** and join the Fan Club for updates on the Fifties Chix book series, more info on your fave characters, secret diary entries, contests, and more!

Also visit the Fifties Chix wiki at

http://fiftieschix.wikispaces.com

for extended activities and fun educational stuff.

BOOK 1

travel to tomorrow

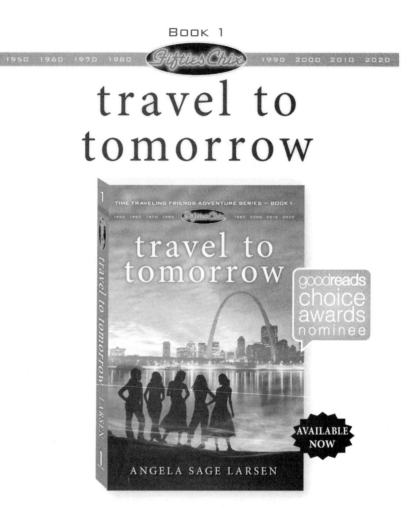

Sock hops. Soda fountains. Slumber parties. Life in 1955 is simple for tomboy Beverly, moody Maxine, high-spirited Judy, studious Mary and artistic Ann. But after a class assignment to predict life in the future, they wake up the next morning in a future they could never have imagined (having time-traveled into a parallel universe to the 21st century. With only each other to trust, they must work together and find their way "home" to 1955; but the more they discover about the future, will they even want to go back?

SIGN UP TO GET UPDATES AND READ SNEAK PREVIEWS OF UPCOMING BOOKS AT FIFTIESCHIX.COM

Book 2

1950 1960 1970 1980 *Fifties Chix* 1990 2000 2010 2020

keeping secrets

THE MYSTERY UNFOLDS IN A FUTURE LINKED TO THE PAST
THROUGH SECRETS THAT MUST NOW BE UNCOVERED AND TOLD.

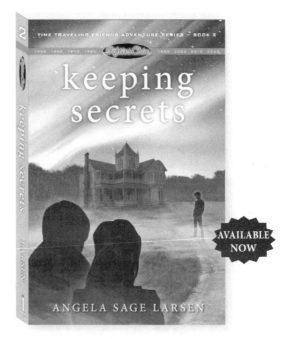

As if their quest to return home isn't challenging enough for Fifties Chix friends Mary, Ann, Judy, Maxine, and Bev – they must also cope with a love triangle between Mary, Ann and James O'Grady; the unexplained disappearance of their classroom teacher; and the revealing essay Maxine writes for the school's underground newspaper.

Hang on tight as the time-traveling quintet explodes through well-kept secrets to find the answers in the second book of the Fifties Chix series.

SIGN UP TO GET UPDATES AND READ SNEAK PREVIEWS OF
UPCOMING BOOKS AT FIFTIESCHIX.COM

COMING SOON!
Books 4 & 5

1950 1960 1970 1980 *Fifties Chix* 1990 2000 2010 2020

broken record
&
till the end of time

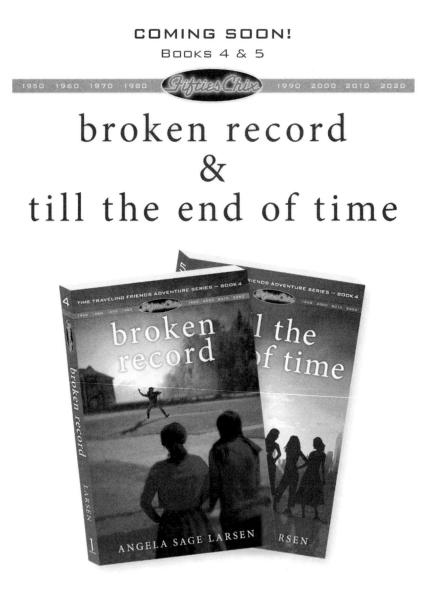

Premiere
http://premiere.fastpencil.com